TO THE RESCUE!

"Mrs. Reg is gone for the week," Max said. "She had to go visit a sick friend who called her yesterday afternoon. She won't be back until Friday, and there are a zillion and one things she left me to do. This is a very busy week. . . . I don't know how I'll ever—"

The phone rang. Max picked it up. He barely said a word, but as soon as he hung up, he dashed back out the door.

"This is our chance, girls," Stevie said. "It gives us a four-day head start on finishing what we started last night. We're going to run Pine Hollow for Max this week while Mrs. Reg is gone. It's the perfect opportunity for the three of us to be everywhere, look everywhere, do everything. If that pin is here, anywhere, we're going to find it."

"And if we don't?" Carole asked.

Stevie shrugged. "Well, then, we will have spent the week earning dozens and dozens of brownie points. How could Max and Mrs. Reg want to kill us when we're indispensable. . . ."

THE SADDLE CLUB

HORSE TROUBLE

BONNIE BRYANT

A BANTAM SKYLARK BOOK®
NEW YORK · TORONTO · LONDON · SYDNEY · AUCKLAND

RL 5, 009–012

HORSE TROUBLE

A Bantam Skylark Book / August 1992

Skylark Books is a registered trademark of Bantam Books,
a division of Bantam Doubleday Dell Publishing Group, Inc.
Registered in U.S. Patent and Trademark Office and elsewhere.

"The Saddle Club" is a trademark of Bonnie Bryant Hiller.
The Saddle Club design/logo, which consists of an inverted
U-shaped design, a riding crop, and a riding hat is a
trademark of Bantam Books.

ISBN 0-553-48025-1

Published simultaneously in the United States and Canada

Bantam Books are published by Bantam Books, a division of Bantam
Doubleday Dell Publishing Group, Inc. Its trademark, consisting of the
words "Bantam Books" and the portrayal of a rooster, is Registered in
U.S. Patent and Trademark Office and in other countries. Marca Regi-
strada. Bantam Books, 666 Fifth Avenue, New York, New York 10103.

PRINTED IN THE UNITED STATES OF AMERICA

OPM   0 9 8 7 6 5 4 3 2

HORSE
TROUBLE

1

LISA ATWOOD FELT great. It was a Monday afternoon, and she'd managed to spend almost every minute of the day at Pine Hollow Stable. She'd spent one hour of that time in a jump class and two hours on a trail ride with her Pony Club, Horse Wise. Summer was her favorite time of year because it meant she could spend a lot of time with horses.

It also meant she could spend a lot of time with friends. Her two best friends, Stevie Lake and Carole Hanson, loved horses just as much as she did. The three of them were all so wild about horses that they had formed their own group, The Saddle Club. There were only two requirements for membership. The first was that the members had to be horse crazy. The second was that they had to be willing to help one another out, no matter what the problem was. When one of the girls got into trouble, two friends were always there to help get her out. Lisa liked that, although she wasn't usually the one who got into trouble.

Even the fact that the girls had all been given chores to do around the stable after class didn't dispel Lisa's happy mood. She knew it was one of the ways Max Regnery, Pine Hollow's owner and chief instructor, kept his expenses down: All the riders pitched in to take care of the animals. Lisa thought it was one of the best things about riding at Pine Hollow. Although she wasn't absolutely wild about mucking out stables, she knew that loving horses meant taking care of them, not just riding them. She was glad to do her part.

Mrs. Reg, Max's mother, was the stable manager. All the young riders adored her, though they weren't too crazy about her habit of assigning chores. If Mrs. Reg saw two girls chatting, she was sure to give them a job while they chatted. Since girls often liked to chat—most especially Stevie, Lisa, and Carole—they often found themselves doing chores like measuring and mixing grains for feed or soaping saddles. This afternoon Mrs. Reg had them moving and checking bales of hay for mold and mildew. It was an important job because moldy hay could make horses sick, but it was difficult and sweaty work on a summer day. The good thing about it now was that it was done, and Lisa was ready to report that fact to Mrs. Reg.

She stepped into Mrs. Reg's office. Mrs. Reg was on the phone, with a serious look on her face. Lisa knew better than to interrupt. Also, from the look on Mrs. Reg's face, she doubted that she *could* interrupt. Mrs. Reg was definitely not aware of her presence. She stepped back out of the office until Mrs. Reg hung up, trying hard not to listen. When she heard the phone put back in its cradle, she reentered. Mrs. Reg looked right up at her. Lisa smiled broadly and saluted.

"The hay-bale task force has completed its inspection, ma'am," she joked. "I'm pleased to report that all of the hay appears to be fresh and mold free!"

Normally Mrs. Reg would like that kind of joking. This time she didn't seem to get it. "Are you sure?" she asked.

Lisa dropped her saluting arm and her pretense. "Of course I'm sure," she said. "We looked over all the bales and everything's fine. No sign of anything amiss. You can trust us, you know."

Mrs. Reg smiled at her then. "I'm sorry, Lisa. I know you know what you're doing. I think I'm sort of distracted. . . ."

Lisa realized it had to be the phone call. Mrs. Reg seemed a little embarrassed, but didn't want to talk about it. That made Lisa feel a little embarrassed, too. She wanted to say something, but she wasn't sure what. Her eyes went to Mrs. Reg's desk, where there was something shining in the afternoon sunlight, and she was very surprised by what she saw.

"What's that?" she asked, looking at a beautiful gold pin.

Mrs. Reg smiled again. "Pretty, isn't it? Go ahead, pick it up."

Lisa did. The pin was of a horse, galloping full out, its tail sailing dramatically behind. It was gold with a brush finish that made the horse seem silky and sleek. And the horse's eye was a diamond that sparkled brightly even in the dim indoor light of Mrs. Reg's office.

"It's not just pretty," Lisa said. "It's *beautiful.*"

"Max gave it to me," Mrs. Reg said. "My Max, I mean." Lisa knew that meant her husband, who had died long ago, not her son, who now ran the stable. "It would be our fortieth wedding anniversary this week. It was his wedding present for me."

Lisa held the pin carefully, turning it, admiring the art and the artistry. She'd seen lots of horse jewelry. The Saddle Club even had its own pin, and she always thought that was pretty, too. But she'd never seen anything as beautiful as this.

"Have Stevie and Carole seen it?" she asked.

"I doubt it," Mrs. Reg said. "I don't usually wear it around here."

Lisa could understand why. A stable was no place for valuables—except horses, of course. "Can I show it to them?"

"Sure," Mrs. Reg said. "I have to talk with Max—*your* Max—about something now. If I'm not here when you bring it back, just put it in my center drawer, okay?"

"Okay, thanks," Lisa said, glad that Mrs. Reg knew she could trust her. That was one advantage to being reliable. People trusted you when it really mattered.

Holding the pin carefully, but not too tightly, she left Mrs. Reg's office and returned to the locker area, where her friends were already changing into their street clothes. They'd made a plan to have a Saddle Club meeting at their favorite hangout, an ice-cream parlor called TD's, right after class. Stevie had said she thought it was a really good idea because she had heard her mother was serving calves' liver for dinner, and she wanted to ruin her appetite.

5

Stevie was like that. She was fun-loving and mischievous. Carole, on the other hand, was the most serious horsewoman of the three of them. She had been riding since she was a very little girl and had long since decided that when she grew up, she would work with horses. All that remained was to decide exactly how she would work with them—whether she'd be a rider, trainer, breeder, veterinarian, instructor, or all of them. When the subject was horses, Carole was all business. On any other subject, she could sometimes be a little flaky.

Lisa was the newest rider of the three, but she'd learned fast, and Max already said she was very good. She was earnest, logical, and methodical about everything she did. She was also a straight-A student and rarely got into trouble, unless dragged there by Stevie.

It always amazed Lisa and her friends how different the three of them were and how much they liked one another in spite of—or perhaps because of—their differences. Of course they had being horse crazy in common, and another thing they shared was an intense dislike of one Veronica diAngelo—a member of their riding class. Veronica was a snooty rich girl who mistakenly believed that because she was rich, she was better than everybody else. The Saddle Club girls thought that she was worse than everybody else, and it had nothing whatsoever to do with her money. It was her basic rotten personality. Lisa wasn't particularly pleased to see that Veronica was in the locker area when she entered to show her friends Mrs. Reg's pin. She held it so that Veronica couldn't see it and sashayed past the girl to her friends. Veronica didn't seem to notice. She was too busy studying her reflection in her compact to see anything but herself. For once Lisa was glad for Veronica's incredible vanity.

"Look at this pin of Mrs. Reg's," Lisa said, holding it out to show her friends.

"Oh, the diamond is so perfect!" Stevie said. "Wouldn't it be wonderful if we could have a pin like that for The Saddle Club?"

Lisa looked at the very special silver horse-head pin on her shirt. She liked Mrs. Reg's pin, but she wouldn't trade her Saddle Club pin for anything. "I don't know . . . ," she began.

"The conformation!" Carole said. Stevie and Lisa stifled giggles. It was just like Carole to look at the characteristics of the horse rather than just the beauty of the jewelry. "And with a head like that, it's got to be an Arabian."

Lisa and Stevie looked again, seeing the pin anew. Of course, Carole was right. The horse was definitely an Arabian—sleek and beautiful.

"What are you looking at?" Veronica asked, suddenly interested. Veronica's own horse was a purebred Arabian mare named Garnet.

Lisa, Stevie, and Carole looked at one another. All had the same thought. Veronica was looking for a way to put them all down. They just *had* to make it impossible for her to do. There was a light in Stevie's eyes.

"Oh, it's just this pin of mine," she said casually, holding it out to Veronica, who took it from her. "Kind of pretty, isn't it?"

Since that was such an obvious understatement, it was enough to silence Veronica for a few seconds while Stevie collected her thoughts. "My brother Chad gave it to me last Christmas," she went on. "It's a nice piece of costume jewelry, don't you think?"

If there was one thing Veronica thought she knew a lot about, it was real jewelry. Telling her that this was fake made it impossible for her to insult the jewelry or Stevie any further. All Veronica could do now was stare at the beautiful pin in her hand, unable to think of anything cutting to say beyond, "Nice, for a fake," which she muttered reluctantly. Stevie beamed proudly.

And then the ruckus began. At first there was just a minor skittering sound, then an unmistakable squeak.

It was followed by a small flash of gray moving quickly across the locker-area floor. That, in turn, was followed by a much larger flash of black and white named Man o' War. The gray was a mouse; the black and white was a cat in hot pursuit.

It was a fact of life that stables have mice. That's why most stables also have cats to keep down the mouse population and Man o' War was just doing his job. The girls, however, and most especially Veronica, wished he were doing it somewhere else.

Veronica leapt up onto the bench and began screaming. The mouse, now even more frightened, ran out from under the bench and stood in the middle of the floor, frozen in terror. It was the opportunity Man o' War had been waiting for. He pounced. That made the mouse move. Fast. That made Veronica scream. That made the cat howl. The mouse fled toward the horse stalls. The cat followed—*very* fast.

That might have been the end of it except that the mouse chose to look for an escape route in the stall of one of the stable's newest horses, an injured and retired racer by the name of Prancer. Lisa knew that most horses have at least one thing that scares them. In the wild such fears protect horses. They know what they have to flee from, and once they know, there's almost nothing that can be done to alleviate that fear.

In Prancer's case, the fear was cats. The moment she spotted Man o' War climbing up and over the doorway to her stall, she began fussing. She whinnied and cried out.

From the sound of the horse's cry, Carole recognized exactly what was happening and that it could be big trouble. Prancer was still recovering from a fracture in her foot that had cost her her career as a racehorse and might well cost her her life if it didn't heal well. A frightened horse could get into awful trouble. She needed to be calmed right away.

"Come on!" she said to her friends. She didn't have to say it twice.

The three girls ran to the stalls and found that the cat had the mouse cornered in the stall. The mouse was stunned by fear; the cat knew he had the upper hand and wasn't about to move. Prancer jumped and kicked, preparing to rear.

Without even thinking about it, Carole and Stevie each grabbed a lead rope. If they could just get the ropes clipped to the horse's halter, they'd have a chance to control her. But there was no way they could go into the stall when she was so upset. Sending one of the three of them off to the hospital wasn't a very good idea.

Stevie and Carole climbed up on the stall door and

tried to reach for the halter. While they did that, Lisa did what she thought was the most logical thing. She took a broom and went into the stall next to Prancer's. That housed a sweet-natured pinto named Patch, who watched all the events going on around him with only mild curiosity. Lisa hiked herself up onto the top of the divider separating the two stalls and reached down with the broom. She could just barely touch the floor of the stall, but that was all she needed. She stretched as far as she could and put the broom right next to the mouse.

This mouse was no fool. Just as Lisa had hoped, he understood that he was in dire straits and immediately scootched into the safety of the broom bristles, holding on for dear life. As soon as Lisa thought she might have the mouse, she lifted the broom back over the divider, left Patch's stall as fast as possible, and took her hostage to the door of the stable, where she shook the broom. A stunned mouse fell out of the bristles. Within half a second he righted himself, looked around, and headed for the tall grass, where Lisa was sure his family was waiting for him. He'd have quite a story to tell them. She paused briefly to wonder how he would explain the miracle of the broom.

When Lisa got back to the stall, however, she found that only half the problem had been solved. The mouse was gone, but Man o' War was still standing in the stall and Prancer was still scared.

"Calm down, girl," Carole was saying. Horses liked to have people talk to them. Prancer particularly liked it when Carole talked to her. The horse seemed to adore Carole, and it was obviously mutual. "Everything's going to be fine. We'll just get that cat out, and you don't have anything to worry about. Poor cat's just as scared as you are."

Lisa looked at the cat. He didn't appear scared, just confused. He couldn't figure out where his dinner had gone!

"Try the broom trick again," Stevie suggested, still trying unsuccessfully to reach for Prancer's halter. For a second Lisa tried to figure out if the cat could possibly hold onto the broom's bristles as the mouse had, but then she realized that wasn't what Stevie meant. She reentered Patch's stall, remounted the divider, and re-reached over with the broom.

The cat saw it coming and he didn't like what he saw. Dodging with his head, he spun a full one hundred eighty degrees and dashed up and out of the stall as fast as he'd dashed into it. Then there was quiet. Prancer looked around, trying to assure herself that the cat was actually gone. Finally the horse relaxed as suddenly as she'd shied. She reached for her hay feeder, grabbed a few strands of sweet hay, and munched. Then she looked up at the three girls still perched on the walls and door of her stall. A quizzical looked crossed the horse's face as if to wonder what on earth all the fuss was about. The girls had been dismissed and they knew it.

"What teamwork!" Lisa said.

"This calls for a celebration," Stevie agreed.

"TD's?" Carole suggested.

It was just what they had in mind.

IT DIDN'T TAKE long before Lisa realized something was wrong. The three girls sat at their favorite booth at TD's and talked about what had happened with Prancer, Man o' War, and the mouse.

"You should have seen the look on that mouse's face when I set him free in the paddock!" Lisa said gleefully. "I mean, his eyes were shining like, like— like . . ." She could see the bright shine in the little creature's eyes, glistening in the outdoor sunlight nearly sparkling. " . . . oh, no."

"Like what?" Stevie asked.

"Diamonds," Lisa said, a look of horror crossing her face. She didn't have to say it again or explain. The moment she uttered the word, her friends knew exactly what she'd just remembered.

"Let's go," Carole said. The girls left TD's in a shot, leaving behind a confused waitress.

"We'll be right back!" Carole called.

"Right after we get out of prison!" Stevie added.

The restaurant door slammed behind them. They didn't even hear it, they were running so fast.

TD's was just a short distance from Pine Hollow. The girls often walked it after class, and it usually took them about ten minutes. This time they covered the distance in less than five minutes—at a run.

"It's got to be in the locker area!" Lisa said breathlessly over her shoulder.

"Yeah," Carole agreed. "That's where it was when we had to save Prancer."

"We'll find it. Don't worry," Stevie said. They all liked the sound of those words. They just hoped they were true.

There was nobody in the locker area when they got there. That wasn't surprising. All the young riders— the only ones who used this room, were long gone. Nobody would be back there until tomorrow. Lisa dropped to her hands and knees to look at the floor. Stevie looked at every surface in the place—tables, benches, and shelves. Carole focused on the tops of the lockers, and when they proved clean (not of dust, just of pins), she began looking in the lockers.

There wasn't a sign of the pin.

The locker area was small, and it didn't take the girls long to be absolutely sure that the pin wasn't there. To be definitely, positively, totally sure, they each switched levels and repeated the search. Then the three of them worked together to move the lockers away from the wall just to see if the pin might have slipped behind them. They found a riding crop there. They didn't find a gold pin with a diamond in it.

"Veronica," Lisa said. "She was the one who was holding it when the cat and the mouse came through. Maybe she took it."

"Veronica would never take a piece of jewelry she thought wasn't real," Stevie said.

"Maybe so, but I think I'd better call her to see if she remembers what happened," Lisa said. Stevie and Carole agreed that was a good idea, and Lisa went to use the phone in Mrs. Reg's office. Normally riders were expected to use the pay phone, but in the case of an emergency, they were allowed to use the stable phone. Lisa thought this qualified as an emergency.

Mrs. Reg's office was empty and dark. When she turned on the light and sat to use the phone, she was struck by the fact that the desk, which had been in its usual state of disorganization when she'd last been in there just over an hour earlier, was now neat as a—she didn't even want to *think* the word—pin. Perhaps Mrs. Reg was turning over a new leaf, Lisa mused quickly as she picked up the phone. Then she cringed as she thought of the more likely answer. Mrs. Reg had straightened everything up looking for her pin. Lisa hated the idea of causing anybody such trouble. She dialed Veronica's number.

Veronica answered the phone herself, which was not surprising since it was her own private telephone line. Lisa explained that the girls had been looking for the horse pin and wondered if Veronica knew what had happened to it.

There was quite a pause. "Pin, pin," Veronica said, repeating the word to remind herself what Lisa was talking about. "Oh, that old pin that Stevie's brother gave her?" At least she remembered it. "I don't know," Veronica went on. "I think I threw the darn thing at the cat. Is that all you want to know?"

It was. Lisa told her so and hung up, now more worried than ever.

"Lisa, is that you?" It was Max. He was surprised to find Lisa in his mother's office.

"I just had to make a call," Lisa said quickly. "I'm sorry, but I didn't have change."

"No problem," Max said. "Just don't tell the whole world I didn't make a fuss, okay?" He grinned at her. Max was really a wonderful person. That made it particularly hard on Lisa, knowing she was lying to him. "Isn't it time for you to get home now?" Max asked. "We want you rested and well for tomorrow's jump class. You're doing very well, you know. I'm awfully flattered. You should be, too."

"Thanks, Max," she said, and in spite of the fact that her mind wasn't on her riding, she was very pleased by his words. Max wasn't usually very free with compliments. "I'm on my way now," she said. "Stevie and Carole are waiting for me. Good night."

She couldn't leave fast enough. There was no point in staying at Pine Hollow. There was nothing there for them. They'd made absolutely sure of that.

The three girls left Pine Hollow for the second time that afternoon. Stevie and Lisa lived near one another. Carole was going home with Stevie because her father was picking her up at Stevie's house instead of at the stable, since he wouldn't be able to get off work for another hour. They didn't talk much as they walked. Stevie had just one question.

"Was Veronica lying?"

Lisa mentally ran through the brief phone conversation again. She would have liked to say she thought

Veronica was lying, but the fact was she was just about certain she wasn't. For one thing, Veronica had a real disdain for fake jewelry. She had a real disdain for anything that didn't cost a lot of money. For another thing, in spite of all the awful things Lisa could say about her—and there were a lot of them—Veronica wasn't a thief.

"No," Lisa said finally. "She really believed the thing was a fake, and she would never be interested in something that wasn't real. Veronica is not the culprit. Trouble is, I don't know who is. I guess that means it's me." Without another word, she split off from Carole and Stevie and headed for her house.

"See you tomorrow," Stevie called after her, trying to sound cheerful. Lisa just grunted in response.

"Poor Lisa," Stevie said. "She just feels awful. I guess I do, too."

"I'm getting a feeling," Stevie said.

"What kind of feeling?" Carole asked.

"I'm getting a feeling that our friend needs our help," Stevie said.

"Yes, it's definitely a Saddle Club project," Carole agreed. "All we have to do is figure out what happened to the pin, find it, and get it back to Mrs. Reg before she notices that it's gone."

"I have a new motto for The Saddle Club," Stevie

said. "'The difficult we do immediately; the impossible takes a little longer.'"

One of the few things Stevie's friends loved most about her was her ability to find something to laugh about in the darkest moments.

"But how *much* longer?" Carole asked. This time she couldn't laugh.

THE NEXT MORNING Lisa was feeling no better about the awful situation than she had the night before.

"Why hasn't Mrs. Reg called?" Lisa asked herself. She stood in front of the mirror in her bathroom, combing her hair and getting ready for the disaster that this day was sure to be. She'd been in front of the mirror, practicing explanations for more than half an hour. None of them seemed adequate, even when paired with her most sincere apologies. And every time she closed her eyes, she saw an image of the pin, gold glinting in the sun, diamond eye sparkling brightly. Now it was gone.

Then she answered her own question. The reason Mrs. Reg hadn't called was that she trusted Lisa. She knew Lisa would never do anything careless with her valuable pin, and she knew that whatever reason Lisa had for not putting it in her drawer last night, as she'd promised, was a good one, and Lisa would be there with the pin in the morning.

Only she wouldn't be. Mrs. Reg was wrong this time. Lisa was not trustworthy. She'd gotten so interested in playing a joke on Veronica and then on chasing a cat and a mouse that she'd forgotten all about a golden horse. She didn't deserve Mrs. Reg's trust, and she knew she would never have it again.

She met Stevie and Carole outside Pine Hollow. Without a word, the three girls entered together and walked straight to Mrs. Reg's office. If they had to face the music, they wanted to get it over with and they wanted to do it together.

Mrs. Reg's office was still dark. The desk was still as neat as a pin. There was nobody there.

"What are you looking for?" Max asked. There was a slight edge to his voice.

"Where's Mrs. Reg?" Lisa asked.

"She's gone for the week," he said. "She had to go visit a sick friend who called her yesterday afternoon. She won't be back until Friday, and there are a zillion and one things she left me to do. This is a very busy week—I'm training a new horse for one of my show riders who expects a perfect mount by Friday—and now I have to manage the stable as well. Never mind that there's a new class beginning and I don't know what else. Mother said something about a list of things that have to get done. I don't know how I'll ever—"

The phone rang. Max picked it up. He barely said a word, but as soon as he hung up, he dashed back out the door.

"This is our chance, girls," Stevie said.

"Chance?" Lisa echoed. "What do you mean? You think this gives us a four-day head start on running out of the country?"

"No," Stevie said. "It gives us a four-day head start on finishing what we started last night. We're going to run Pine Hollow for Max this week while Mrs. Reg is gone. Don't you see? It's going to be the perfect opportunity for the three of us to be everywhere, look everywhere, do everything. If that pin is here, anywhere, we're going to find it."

"And if we don't?" Carole asked.

Stevie shrugged. "Well, then, we will have spent the week earning dozens and dozens of brownie points. How could Max and Mrs. Reg want to kill us when we're indispensable?"

Lisa and Carole considered the situation. Stevie's suggestion had some merit. It was also a whole lot better than the explanations and apologies that Lisa had been practicing, and it had the benefit of possibly accomplishing what appeared to be the impossible—finding the pin.

"It's worth trying," Lisa said.

Carole thought so, too. She thought about how hard the week would be as they tried to keep up a full schedule of classes and chores, plus manage the stable *and* find the pin. They would certainly be exhausted by the time Friday rolled around. She had an idea.

"Then, after it's all over" (and we've been banished from Pine Hollow for life, she thought, but did not say), "why don't you plan to come to my house on Friday for a dinner and a sleepover? I promised Dad I'd cook for him, and I want to try a new recipe I saw for vegetable lasagna—"

"I'll make Rice Krispie treats," Stevie suggested. It was one thing she was really good at cooking.

"I think we should plan for crow on the menu," Lisa said glumly.

"No way," Stevie said. "I think Carole's right. We should be looking on the bright side of things. We're going to do a wonderful job of managing the stable *and* we're going to find the pin."

"First thing is convincing Max to let us do Mrs. Reg's job," Lisa said.

Lisa and Carole both looked at Stevie. She had a lot of experience trying to convince Max of things. In this case they all thought it would be easy.

"Oh, Ma-ax!" she called out as he dashed by. "I've got some good news for you!"

3

ONCE CLASSES WERE over and their horses were groomed and fed, The Saddle Club was ready to begin the real work of the day—filling in for Mrs. Reg.

Stevie was the first one to change into street clothes, and so she was the first to arrive at Mrs. Reg's office. By the time Carole and Lisa got there, just a few seconds later, their friend had already ensconced herself in Mrs. Reg's chair and had it tilted back. Her feet were propped up on the desk.

"It's a good thing she doesn't have a cigar," Lisa teased. "She'd be trying to pretend she was some sort of mogul!"

"Ah, but I have a riding crop!" Stevie reminded her,

slapping it sharply against her thigh. "That's almost as good—maybe even better."

"Let's forget the status symbols and get to work," Carole said. "I think there's a lot to do."

Stevie removed her feet from Mrs. Reg's desk and set the chair back upright. She leaned forward and pulled the single piece of paper on the desk toward her.

"A list," she announced. "Just like Max said."

"And what does it say?" Carole asked.

"What have we gotten ourselves in for?" Lisa added.

Stevie crinkled her forehead thoughtfully.

" 'Painting, front of stable,' " she read.

The girls were quiet.

"That's a big job," Carole said.

"But it's just the *front*," Stevie said. "That's the side by the driveway. That's not big."

An image of the horse pin went through Lisa's mind. It made her realize that they just *had* to do Mrs. Reg's job, no matter how tough it might be. "You're right," she said to Stevie. "It's not big. No problem. We can get some ladders—"

Carole was swept up by their enthusiasm. "I remember when they painted the whole thing a couple of years ago. The leftover paint is stored in the utility shed by the grain shed. I'm sure there's enough left there to just do the front."

"Tomorrow," Stevie said. "We can do it after class."

"Tomorrow," they agreed. It didn't seem so hard after all.

"What's next on the list?" Lisa asked. "Redo the roof?"

"No, the next thing is much easier. It says there's going to be a new class of four beginners on Wednesday at eight o'clock. It says something here about a team and Red's going to do the class. They're also scheduled for an afternoon trail ride. Busy little kids, huh?" Stevie remarked.

"It's always a good idea to have a class start out thinking of themselves as a team," Carole said. "They work together, they learn together. I'll take care of getting the ponies ready for them tomorrow morning," she volunteered. "Dad already said he was going to have to drop me off early, so I'll be here by seven-thirty at the latest. I can saddle up four ponies first thing tomorrow."

"Check!" Stevie said. "See, this really is easy. Next says 'Buy food for Friday.'"

"I noticed that we were running low on grain when we checked the bales of hay yesterday," Lisa said.

"Well, not really low, but I suppose Mrs. Reg is just being careful."

Stevie scratched her head. The easiest way to solve this problem would be to ask Max what to order and where to order it from. However, their whole point in taking on these jobs was to keep Max from having to think about these things. *They* were being the stable managers, not he. She scratched again, harder.

"I've got it," she said. "Whenever anybody delivers anything, there are papers. Somewhere around here Mrs. Reg must have an invoice or something from the last delivery. I'll just call the same place and make the same order. If the stuff was okay the last time, it's going to be fine this time, too. The hardest part may be getting it here by Friday."

Carole looked proudly at her friend Stevie. It was nice that she could figure out how to cope with something that seemed so tricky. "Nice thinking," she said, and she meant it.

"So what's next on the list?" Lisa asked. She was beginning to get the feeling it was her turn to volunteer to solve a tricky problem.

"Wow," Stevie said, looking up from the list. "It looks like we've got a VIP coming to Pine Hollow."

"Who's that?" Lisa asked. This could be interesting.

"The French ambassador *himself*! It says here, 'Thursday, 11, Am. French. One-hour trail ride.'"

"That seems odd," Carole said. "I didn't know we had an ambassador in town."

"What's so odd about it?" Lisa challenged. "Remember when the Brazilian ambassador was here?"

Lisa had a point. Pine Hollow was located in Willow Creek, Virginia, just twenty miles from Washington, D.C. There were a lot of people who lived in town and worked in Washington. Although most of the people involved in government work were Americans, many of them did come from other countries and work in embassies and other offices like international cultural organizations. The Brazilian ambassador and his family had lived right in Willow Creek. The girls also remembered a French diplomat's daughter who had ridden at Pine Hollow for a brief time. Her name was Estelle. Lisa had befriended her and invited her to join The Saddle Club before she'd realized that Estelle was a liar. Lisa had always felt bad about what had happened. This seemed to her to be an opportunity to make it up to her friends.

"I'll take care of that," she said. "I'm getting an A in French—"

"So what else is new?" Stevie teased.

Lisa blushed and then defended herself. "Well, this time it looks like it may do me some good. Anyway, I need some practice with my French. I'll go for a trail ride with the French ambassador."

"*Merci beaucoup,*" Stevie said graciously. Then she turned to Carole. "And since Lisa is solving that problem, you get to cope with the fact that somebody named Jarvis is coming Thursday at one P.M. and wants his 'favorite horse.' That's what Mrs. Reg wrote."

"The problem with that is, Mrs. Reg always remembers who wants what horse. She assigns horses to the riders for every class," Carole said. "Max did that today, but I think we should do it starting tomorrow. I don't mind taking on that job. But I have to remember to ask Max who Mr. Jarvis's favorite horse is."

"Okay, and it makes sense for you to take on the horse assignments," Stevie said, nodding agreement. "You know the horses and the riders the best. It's a deal, and that's the last of the list."

"Piece of cake—uh, *gâteau,*" Lisa said, quickly translating "cake" into French.

Once the jobs had been assigned, it seemed to be time to begin the other part of their job as stable managers—finding Mrs. Reg's pin.

"The only place we searched yesterday was the

locker area," Carole said. "I've been thinking about it, and I think it's possible one of the cats found the pin where Veronica threw it and may have begun playing with it. You know how they are, right?"

The girls did know. They'd often seen the cats at the stable begin playing with something that wasn't a mouse. A cat could take almost anything—a pencil, marble, piece of straw—and bat it all over the place.

"The tack room!" Lisa said.

"That place is a mess!" Stevie said.

"Exactly," Carole said.

In the utility closet they found two brooms and a mop, just what they would need to probe around on the dark and shadowy floor of the tack room, where they hoped they'd find Mrs. Reg's pin. Lisa organized them. She got Carole and Stevie to begin in opposite corners, on their hands and knees, examining and sweeping every single inch of the floor as they moved toward one another. It wasn't an easy job. The tack room not only had tack hanging from every inch of wall all the way around it, it also had racks and hooks lined up in the center of the room to house saddles and bridles. There were also the upper shelves, where the specialized saddles were kept, along with the tack for the wagons and the sleigh. Lisa had decided they could omit the shelves and the loft because it was unlikely that a cat would carry the pin that high. After all, real gold was heavy, certainly heavier than a mouse. It might be fun to bat around the floor, but it would be downright dangerous for a cat to carry it up a ladder in his mouth.

"Got something!" Stevie said excitedly. She could hear the wonderful sound of metal being dragged across the old floorboards by her broom. She maneuvered the broom carefully because she couldn't see what she was pulling toward her. She could only hear it, and her ears told her it was good news. Her ears were wrong. When the broom brought her quarry into the light, Stevie saw that it wasn't a gold pin, it was a steel snaffle bit.

"False alarm," she said.

In the opposite corner, Carole took her turn. She stuck the broom back into the dark corner under what seemed to be a curtain of leather straps hanging from the wall hooks. She brought the broom back toward her. It came back empty. It wasn't actually completely empty. She had a significant dust bunny and something that looked like an old wad of gum. She also found a sponge with the remains of some saddle soap on it. She tried to imagine what would induce somebody to lose a saddle-soap sponge in the farthest, darkest corner of the tack room. She decided it must have been frustration—a feeling she suspected she was going to learn too much about in the next few days.

Lisa wasn't having any more luck than her friends. While they worked on the floor, she studied the morass of leathers and combed through the buckets of metal pieces, S-hooks, snap locks, curb chains, and the like. Tack seemed to be made up of equal parts of leather and metal, so there was an awful lot of metal in the room, but none of it was eighteen-karat gold.

The girls were too busy at their jobs to notice the arrival of Max Regnery. He cleared his throat to announce his presence.

They looked up. He stood by the door with his hands on his hips and a smile on his face.

"When you girls fill in for my mother, you really fill in! I never saw her cleaning the tack room. What happened? You couldn't find any unsuspecting riders with free time on their hands?" He laughed at his own joke.

It surprised Lisa to find that Max was actually amused by his mother's habit of assigning jobs to people who happened not to be frantically busy when she saw them.

"Very funny," Stevie said, recovering from her surprise and rising from her knees. "Actually, though, it's just that this really needed to be done, and we knew there was nobody who would do a better job than we will. So we're doing it. You wouldn't believe the dirt we're finding."

"And the sponges," Carole said.

Max looked at her quizzically. Whatever he wanted to ask or say, he decided to skip it. Some questions were best left unasked. He cleared his throat again. "Well, then, um, I'll let you girls get back to work. I'm taking a group out onto the trail. I won't be back for a while. I'll see you tomorrow."

"Oh, speaking of tomorrow," Carole said. "There's a new class beginning at eight o'clock. Did you know about that? I'll take care of tacking up their mounts when I get here early."

"I do know about them," Max said. "I have to be in town all morning. Red's taking the class for me. I wish I could be here. I like that team, but I can't. I'll tell Red you'll have the riders' horses ready. Thanks."

"No problem," Carole said. "We're just trying to be helpful."

"I can tell," Max said. "I'll be back by ten o'clock. See you all in jump class. Good-bye for now."

"Bye," Lisa said. She then turned her attention back to the buckets arrayed in front of her. Carole and Stevie reached their brooms back under the leathers. The girls worked in silence, each hoping for the sound of metal—specifically gold.

"Oh, look, the three blind mice," Veronica diAngelo said, walking into the tack room to deposit Garnet's tack on its rack. "Usually you're running *away* from work, but now that Mrs. Reg is gone, you three can't work hard enough to impress Max, can you?"

Once again Veronica had managed to astonish Lisa. It stunned her to realize how far from the truth Veronica was. Actually, she realized a second later, it was very logical. Veronica always did everything she could to get out of doing work that Mrs. Reg assigned, and also always tried, whenever it wasn't much effort, to impress Max. She naturally assumed that others had the same motivations she did. Lisa certainly didn't want to tell Veronica the truth, so she did the only other sensible thing—she agreed with her.

"You're so right, Veronica," she said. "And Max has already noticed our good work. He was so impressed that the next thing you know, he'll have us painting the stable! Want to help?"

"Hah!" Veronica said. She knew an exit line when she heard one. She was gone in a flash.

It provided a moment of laughter, but it was only a brief one. The girls had a lot of work to do and little time to do it. However, an hour later they were reluctantly concluding that the time had not been well spent. All they had to show for their work was a substantial pile of things they'd found on the floor that now had to be thrown out or put away. It wasn't what they'd had in mind when they'd begun cleaning the tack room. The worst part was that the tack room didn't look any cleaner for its careful dusting.

"Let's go, girls," Lisa said, putting her dust mop back in the utility closet.

"Fiddle-dee-dee," Stevie said as she put the broom next to Lisa's mop. "Tomorrow will be another day!"

That's just what they were all afraid of.

4

SINCE CAROLE LOVED *everything* about horses, it was difficult for her to choose what she loved most. High up on her list after riding them, though, were the quiet moments spent alone in a stable surrounded by horses. It made her feel more at one with them. This morning was no exception. She'd arrived at Pine Hollow before seven. Max was in town with his errands. Mrs. Reg was still at her friend's house, and Red hadn't arrived yet. The place was totally quiet, except for the comfortable sounds of horses, munching on hay, chomping on grain, the occasional stomp of a hoof on a straw-covered floor, a relaxed snort, a whinny.

"Good morning, boys and girls," Carole said, chatting easily to the ponies, who were all housed near one another. Nickel stuck his head up over the door to his stall. Carole patted his soft nose.

There were four riders coming in the beginners' class. Carole decided to tack up Nickel, Dime, Quarter, and Penny for the class. Pine Hollow, a stable filled with traditions, had the tradition of naming its ponies after coins—small change. Carole liked that tradition. The young riders always got a kick out of that, too. She was looking forward to seeing the smiles on the faces of the stable's newest riders when they arrived in forty-five minutes.

Carole began the process of tacking up the ponies. Ponies were smaller than horses; the usual definition of a pony was that it had to be less than 14.2 hands, measured at the pony's withers. A hand was four inches—the approximate width of a man's hand across the knuckles—and the .2 meant two inches. Thus a pony was no taller than fifty-eight inches from the floor to the area at the base of its mane, called the withers. Because they were relatively small, ponies were ideal mounts for young beginners. They did everything full-sized horses did; they were just smaller and less likely to frighten a new rider.

Although ponies were small, they needed the same

amount of tack as horses, so it took Carole more than half an hour to tack up four of them. When she was done, all four ponies were ready and seemed eager to meet their new riders. One by one Carole led the ponies to the paddock near the front of the stable so they could greet the riders when they arrived. They would be such a welcoming sight that Carole was sure these youngsters would be as thrilled with riding as she was. Another thing Carole loved about horses was being able to share the joy of them with others. This seemed like a wonderful opportunity to do that.

Carole climbed up onto the paddock fence and waited to welcome the new beginners. She almost wished she didn't have a class coming up right away. She was eager to introduce the kids to the ponies, show them how to climb into their saddles, teach them how to hold their riding crops and everything else that first-timers needed to know.

She could almost see the smiles on their faces and hear their excited giggles. Carole loved to watch little girls and boys in their brand-new riding clothes—boots without a scratch, pants that are a little loose so the girls can grow into them—actually sitting in a saddle for the first time. Carole sighed contentedly just thinking about it all. She was so involved in her own daydream that she never even saw Red O'Malley walk over to her, followed by four extremely tall men in riding clothes.

"Morning, Carole," Red said. "Max told me you were taking care of tacking up horses for the new class today."

"Yep," Carole said proudly. "I've got Nickel, Penny, Quarter, and Dime all ready and raring to go. The kids ought to be here any minute." She looked at her watch. It was already eight o'clock. "Funny. They should already be here."

One of the men standing near Red cleared his throat. "They *are* already here," he said.

Carole looked at him. A fog began to clear, and she didn't much like what she saw. In front of her were four very large men. Behind her were four very small ponies. This wasn't a class of beginning children riders. These were definitely grown-ups—and very big ones at that. Then she remembered that Mrs. Reg's note had said something about a "team," and Max had used the same word. One more look and she didn't have to ask the question. She knew what the word "team" meant. These men were basketball players from the local professional team. They were well over six feet tall. One of them was probably seven feet tall, and Carole had saddled up the stable's smallest ponies for them!

She wanted to die.

One of the men started laughing.

"I thought we were supposed to do the riding, but if these little fellows need to go somewhere, I guess we could carry them," another said.

Red laughed, too.

"I'd thought—" Carole began, but she couldn't go on. Everybody knew what she'd thought. She didn't need to explain. She just felt terribly embarrassed. She also could imagine what her father—a big basketball fan—was going to say when he heard about her mistake.

Since dying didn't seem to be a real option right then, Carole decided that her only other choice was to correct her mistake. She slid down from the fence and unhitched two ponies to return them to their stalls. Then, at just exactly the right minute, Stevie and Lisa arrived. One glance and they knew what they had to do. They each took a lead rope and followed Carole into the stable. Without discussion the girls saddled up Pine Hollow's four tallest horses and had them hitched in the paddock within ten minutes.

All images of the joyful faces of happy children and

the gleeful giggles of young learners had fled from Carole's mind. The only thing she wanted to see was the backs of four very tall men on four very tall horses disappearing around the far side of the stable where she couldn't see them laughing at her silly mistake. Carole didn't like to appear ridiculous, but she thought she'd done an awfully good job of it that morning. She cringed as she held the horses' leads while the men mounted, and she shuddered with relief when Red finally led the group to the ring.

"Thank you," she whispered to her friends.

"Oh, you're welcome," Lisa said.

"No problem," Stevie agreed. "I got the feeling that this was the funniest thing that had happened to those guys in a long time. They *loved* it."

Carole gave her a withering look. Stevie realized that Carole did not see the humor. She hadn't loved it at all.

"Shouldn't we be tacking up our own horses for class?" Lisa asked.

"And *untacking* the ponies," Carole said pointedly. Not only had she made an awful mistake, but she'd also caused herself and her friends a lot of unnecessary work. No matter how funny the men thought it was and no matter how lightly Lisa and Stevie took it, the whole thing upset Carole a lot.

She was calmer, but still upset, when her class began. On Wednesdays they began their day with drill work, followed by jump class. These were two things Carole loved. She loved the precision of trying to make her horse do just exactly what she told him to do so he would be coordinated with the other horses. It was a challenge for her horse, Starlight, who tended to be a little resentful of very structured activities, but that was a challenge Carole was usually willing to meet. This day she found she wasn't so willing, and as a result, Starlight was even less willing. She had to take him out of the drill and work with him alone until he was calmed down, but she knew that it wasn't Starlight who needed calming; it was Carole.

Jump class was even worse. By then Max was back and he'd heard about Carole's mix-up from Red. Since the basketball players thought it was funny, Max thought it was funny. He thought it was funny enough to tease her about it so that although only a few people had known at the beginning of the class, by the time Carole had been asked to take Starlight over a few jumps that were just one inch high, everybody knew and was laughing.

"They're not laughing at you," Stevie said. "They're laughing at the situation."

It didn't make Carole feel any better. By lunchtime

she found herself actually looking forward to painting the stable. At least she could be on a ladder so high above everybody else that she couldn't see them laugh.

WHEN THREE O'CLOCK came around, The Saddle Club groomed their horses and put them back into their stalls for the day. Class was done, it was time for the real work to begin.

Stevie had a list. It read: paint, brushes, ladders. Lisa also had a list. It read: paint (red and white), pans, brushes, ladder, turpentine, hats, drop cloths, tape.

Carole looked at both lists. It confirmed her suspicion that Lisa was a better list maker than Stevie.

"I'm sure all this stuff is in the utility shed," Carole said. The three girls went there and found that Carole was right.

Carole found the cans of paint and stacked them for ease of carrying. Lisa found the pans, brushes, turpentine, tape, hats, and drop cloths—

"What do we need drop cloths for?" Stevie asked. "We're painting outside, not inside. Do we really have to protect the ground?"

"You never know," Lisa said, sounding very much as if she did, in fact, know. Then, to prove it, she spread one of the drop cloths out, put all the equipment onto it, and then folded up the corners of the drop cloth so she could use it as a carrying bag. Stevie thought that sometimes Lisa was almost *too* organized for her own good.

Stevie spotted the folding ladder and picked it up. It was long and awkward, but it wasn't awfully heavy, and she found that as long as she held it in the middle, she could manage it. The three girls walked together back toward the stable.

As they walked, it occurred to Stevie that it was just about perfect painting weather. The sun was bright; the sky was cloudless. It wasn't too hot and it wasn't humid. There was something about the lovely summer day that made Stevie feel good. She wasn't alone either. Out of the corner of her eye, she spotted Pepper, an old retired horse, positively frolicking in his pasture.

"Oh, look at that!" she said, turning to watch.

Her sudden movement accomplished several things. It gave Stevie a better view of Pepper, but it also made the ladder turn with her, knocking both of her friends off their feet.

"Oomph!"

"Watch—"

"Oh, sorry," Stevie said when she saw what she had done. She turned back, much more carefully than she'd turned around in the first place.

"That's quite a weapon," Lisa remarked, looking warily at the ladder.

"In the right hands," Carole said pointedly.

"You guys okay?" Stevie asked. She really hadn't meant to hurt her friends, and she felt bad about it.

"We will be as long as we don't walk next to you again!" Lisa said. She wasn't hurt, but she was more than a little annoyed that Stevie's mistake had made her drop everything she was carrying, and now three painter's hats were blowing across the pasture toward Pepper.

"I'll get them!" Stevie offered, once again swinging around so she could see where they were going. Lisa and Carole dived for cover—this time managing to get out of the way of the swirling ladder.

"*I'll* get the hats," Lisa said. "And Stevie, you walk ahead—*way* ahead."

Sheepishly Stevie agreed.

5

"LOOK, ALL WE have to do is put some white paint on the white parts and some red paint on the red parts. What's so hard about that?"

Stevie's own words echoed in her head. It had all seemed so easy when she said it, but now she appeared to be very busy putting the white parts on the red parts and vice versa, and the overall effect was definitely more *pink* than anything else.

"Grrrrr!" she commented.

Lisa and Carole were beneath her at ground level. Stevie had claimed the ladder, thinking it would be fun to be up high. What it really was, was harder. Every time she needed something, she had to step down, and the ladder wobbled in a very unpleasant way.

"Trouble up there?" Lisa asked, looking at Stevie's scrowl.

"I'd like to be able to say that I'm seeing red," Stevie said sardonically. "However, it seems to be more like pink. . . ."

Lisa stepped back and looked up. Stevie had a point. The stable was definitely taking on a pink hue, and that wasn't what was supposed to happen.

"I did the white and then I did the red, but the white got mixed in with the red and the red with the white, and I think I'd better not make any long-term plans to be a house painter."

Lisa squinted to see what was causing the problem. She was such a logical person that she didn't always understand when other people weren't as logical as she was. Stevie was a special problem in that regard! Then she figured it out.

"Masking tape," she said. "You need masking tape."

"I do?" Stevie asked.

"Definitely," Lisa said. "See, first you paint all the red parts, more or less trying to avoid the white ones, but if you get some red on those, it's okay. When the red is dry, you put tape around the edges of the white and you paint the white. So then, if you slosh a little over the edges, all you're painting is the tape, not the red. When the white is dry, you remove the tape and *bingo,* it's perfect."

"It is?" Stevie was not convinced.

"Try it," Lisa said. She handed up a roll of tape.

Stevie looked at the parts that Lisa had already done, and she had to admit that they looked an awful lot better than what she was working on. She put down the brush with white paint and picked up the one with red paint. She began again, blotting out all the pink with red. It looked better immediately. Stevie painted with renewed enthusiasm.

"Well, if it isn't the three blind mice again," Veronica said icily. "Scurrying like crazy, trying to impress Max again, huh?"

"Watch it, Veronica," Stevie said from above. "We're armed." She held her red paintbrush menacingly above Veronica's head. The idea of red splatters on her designer breeches and jacket was more than Veronica could stand. She dashed off. The Saddle Club was not sorry to see her go. They resumed their work.

Lisa found that she had developed a rhythm to her strokes. Up down, up down, shift to the right, up down, up down, time to refill the brush. Up down, up down . . . It went quickly enough, and the results were good. The trouble was that it was tiring for her arm. She shifted the paintbrush to her left hand and resumed her work. That was okay for a while. Then she spent more time taping around the white sections on parts of the red that were already dry. That was when a sound caught her ear. It was the playful whinny of a horse romping in a paddock. Then she remembered.

"Diablo," she said. Carole and Stevie looked at her. "I left him in the paddock after class," she explained. "He seemed to need more of a cool-down than I had time to give him, so I just set him loose in the paddock. I thought that would help."

"He's probably cooled down by now," Carole said. "Why don't you take a break and bring him into the stable."

Those were the very words Lisa's weary arm had been waiting to hear. That way she could take a break, but still be doing something useful. "Okay," she agreed.

Diablo sniffed curiously as Lisa approached him with a lead rope. At first she thought he was sniffing at her, but then she realized that the smell of paint seemed to be alerting him. Lisa had often wondered what was on a horse's mind, and she did so again. Horses often had early warning systems that told them something dangerous was around, even when there wasn't anything dangerous at all. Prancer's fear of cats was like that. Diablo seemed to be nervous about the smell of paint. Lisa spoke to calm him.

"Don't worry, boy, there's nothing to fear. We're just doing a little work for Mrs. Reg. It won't be long, and then imagine how nice the stable is going to look—at least from the front. Your home is going to be so beautiful that you'll be proud to invite your friends to come see it."

She knew the horse couldn't understand a word she was saying, but she also knew that he understood her tone of voice and that was all that mattered. Reassured, Diablo followed her to the stable. She kept chatting all the while.

"And when I put you in your stall, I'm going to give you some fresh hay and water, and that'll be so delicious and smell so good, you won't even notice the paint, will you?"

Lisa was totally occupied with her chattering. She was too occupied to notice what Stevie was doing on top of the ladder as she and Diablo approached. Stevie had peeled out a yard-long piece of masking tape. It was too long and immediately became an unruly tangle. As she tried to untangle it, it stuck onto the cloth she'd been using to wipe her hands and her brushes. Then the tape attached to the brush with red paint.

"Oh, drat!" Stevie said, trying to loosen everything from the mass of tape.

Lisa didn't see any of this. Diablo saw it all. Lisa tugged at his lead rope, bringing him right between the legs of the folding ladder where Stevie was perched at just the moment when Stevie shook the sticky tangled mess of tape, rag, and brush most vigorously. It was all Diablo could take. He didn't exactly rear, though he came close to it. He shied and he bucked. It was just enough to jiggle the ladder seriously, and when that happened, something else happened, too. Two paint buckets, once carefully balanced on the ladder's shelf, became unbalanced and toppled over.

Lisa had already passed under the ladder. Most of Diablo had not. Much to the horse's dismay—to say nothing of the girls'—his rear half was drenched by the toppled red and white paint. It was all he could take. He bolted. Lisa was so astonished that she simply let go of the lead rope and watched helplessly while he fled right through the stable, out the other side, and into the paddock at the back of the stable. Normally that would be enough to contain him, but not in his frightened state. Diablo took one look at the paddock fence and flew right over it.

Stevie growled again. Lisa hollered "Stop him!" but there was nobody there to stop him, and even if there had been, he was too frightened to be stopped. When it came to horse trouble, Carole was the most logical thinker in the group. She put down her paintbrush.

"I'll take Starlight out and catch Diablo," she said. "He'll stop running pretty soon, and I know he's going to be easy to find."

"Sure," Lisa said, dismayed. "How many horses are there out in the field dressed as a clown?"

"He did look pretty funny, you know," Stevie said, trying to emphasize the absurdity of it all. The humor was lost on Lisa. She gave Stevie a withering look. Stevie realized this might not be the best time to try to joke about what had happened. From the look on Lisa's face, it seemed that sometime in the future— like fifty years into the future—would be a better time. She turned her paint buckets back upright, took her brush in her hand, and resumed painting. She reminded herself that as long as Carole was going to fetch Diablo, the best thing she could do was paint. Lisa didn't say anything. She just picked up her paintbrush and got back to work, too.

Carole took off her painter's hat and went to Starlight's stall. She was always glad for an excuse to ride her horse, and this seemed an especially nice time, since it gave her an opportunity to be away from a guilty Stevie and an angry Lisa. She hoped they'd both be in better moods by the time she got back.

She didn't want to take the time to tack up Starlight. She decided to ride him bareback. She slipped a bridle on him, led him to the rear door of the stable—away from the painters—and hopped onto his back. Riding Starlight bareback was always a special joy. It made her feel closer to her horse and closer to the origins of riding. After all, the first riders had hardly had choices between English and Western saddles, pads and blankets. They just sat on their horses' backs and rode. Now that was what Carole was doing, too. She felt the strong and supple horse beneath her, and with every step she pulled farther and farther away from everything that had gone wrong—the ponies and the basketball players, the dreadful drill class, the embarrassing jump class, the miserable painting job they were doing, the horrible paint spill on poor old Diablo.

Starlight seemed to sense Carole's need for freedom and liberation from the less-than-perfect day. He took a deep breath and lengthened his stride, moving more quickly, more surely, as his rider directed him.

It didn't take Carole long to spot Diablo. For one thing, he was the only red-and-white horse in the field. For another, he was the only horse in the field at all. He seemed unaware of the new color he'd taken on, and he was munching quietly at the sweet grass. Starlight picked up a trot and approached him. Diablo lifted his head when he heard the other horse approaching. Apparently that was enough quiet munching for Diablo. Another possibility was that he recognized Carole as one of the people who had covered him with paint, and he didn't want anything more to do with her. He moved away.

Carole drew in Starlight's reins. He slowed to a walk while Carole thought about the situation. If Diablo didn't want to be caught, she and Starlight had two choices. The first was to be patient and wait for Diablo to change his mind, approaching him slowly all the time. The other was to try to chase him down. Carole opted for patience. Starlight stopped about twenty feet from Diablo. Diablo seemed a little nervous at first, but once he became convinced he wasn't being chased, he turned his attention to the grass at his feet. Carole had Starlight take another few steps. Diablo took a few steps, too. Carole stopped. She waited and then she tried again. This time she and Starlight closed the gap to fifteen feet. She waited and tried again. Starlight took three steps, Diablo took only two. It was slow, but it was working. Carole waited some more and tried again. She found that if she watched Diablo's ears very carefully, she could tell when he was relaxed enough for her to approach him just a little bit.

She was less than six feet from the horse when a group of riders appeared at the edge of the field. Diablo's ears perked up alertly. He lifted his head. This horse had already had as much trauma as he could take for one day. Five more horses, with riders who might or might not be planning something for him, were just too much for Diablo. He took off and fled, and at that moment all of Carole's patience fled, too. She took the only other option open to her. She raced after him.

Diablo tore across the field, challenging the trail riders by racing right at them. At first Carole saw only that there were five riders and that one of them was Red O'Malley. All of her concentration was on the red-and-white-splattered horse ahead of her. Then the sound of laughter distracted her enough to make her look at exactly who those riders were. Her second look was all it took, for she could see that all of them, except Red, were very, very tall. The beginners' class of basketball players had apparently talked Red into a follow-up trail ride, and they were enjoying themselves immensely—at Carole's expense.

That was when Carole stopped seeing red and white speckles and began to see only red. She was only trying to do the very best job she could, and it seemed that the harder she tried, the bigger mistakes she made and the more these men ended up laughing at her. She was furious!

Beneath her, Starlight felt a sudden change in her mood and her position. Starlight always tried to please Carole, and so he wanted to do what he thought she wanted. He didn't always do the right thing, but this time he did. Without further urging, he began moving faster and more surely in pursuit of the frantic Diablo. Once Starlight was committed, it didn't take long. Carole and Starlight flew past the laughing riders. She never looked back—just concentrated totally on the loose horse in front of her. Diablo tried dodging, he tried running, he tried doubling back. None of it worked. Starlight had him in his sights, and Carole was totally determined to win. Within a few minutes Starlight had come up alongside the fleeing bay. Carole reached over and grabbed the dangling lead rope. Without further instruction Starlight did exactly the right thing. He watched Diablo out of one eye and matched his own pace to Diablo's. Carole tugged gently on the lead rope. Diablo wanted to run some more, but he was a well-trained horse and knew a sharp signal when he felt one. He slowed. Starlight slowed as well. Diablo slowed some more. So did Starlight. Soon Starlight and Diablo were walking. Carole began speaking to the frightened horse.

"Don't worry, boy. We're going to take care of you. We'll get you back to the stable and see if we can't get some of that nasty paint off you. We'll get you some hay and some grain and a nice bucket of fresh water. You'll have your friends nearby, and not a one of them will dare make fun of you. Nobody's going to laugh at you at all."

Diablo listened to Carole. Even though he couldn't understand the words, he understood the tone. Carole spoke to him the entire way back to the stable—even as she passed Red and the basketball players. She knew that as long as she was talking to the horse, they wouldn't try to say anything to her. As she passed, however, she did hear Red explaining her chatter to the tall men.

"She's calming the horse down," Red said, "and she knows exactly what she's doing."

"She *does?*" one of the men asked, sounding rather astonished. The other three began laughing.

For the second time that day, Carole wanted to die. Instantly.

CAROLE WENT DIRECTLY to the stalls with Starlight and Diablo. She called out to Stevie and Lisa to let them know that she was back and had Diablo. She didn't want to be anywhere in public where anyone, especially four basketball players, one head stable hand, and one stable owner, might see her and start laughing at all the foolish things she'd done all day long. Animals were more forgiving than people. The horses, even Diablo, seemed happy for her company.

She removed Starlight's bridle, gave him a quick brushing, and set him loose in his stall. She'd already groomed him once that day, and that should be enough. Diablo was going to be more of a challenge. She found some old rags and began working on the paint. It was oil-based, fast-drying outdoor paint. It didn't want to come off at all. She knew she could use turpentine on it, but that stuff was very abrasive and could harm the horse's skin. Since Diablo tended to have sensitive skin, she thought it was a bad idea. Moreover, turpentine was very flammable, and she didn't like the idea of using something very flammable in the stable where fire was always a danger. Finally, the thought of the strong, unpleasant odor filling the stable was enough to convince her not to use turpentine. She rubbed, she washed, she brushed, she combed. She actually got some paint off, but not much. After working on it for fifteen minutes, she decided that it would be no worse tomorrow, when she could work on it outdoors and use some turpentine carefully.

"Sorry about that, Diablo," she said, patting his shoulder affectionately. "For now you're just going to have to live with it. Tomorrow Stevie and Lisa and I will begin work on your make-over. We'll get you back to a nice glistening brown, okay?"

He nuzzled her and tickled her neck. "If that's an apology for your misbehavior, I accept it," she said, and hugged him back. At least Diablo didn't seem to be inclined to laugh at her. She gave him fresh hay and water and a ration of grain for his supper.

She found the four basketball players' horses in the paddock by the stable's rear door, waiting to be untacked and put up for the night. When there was work to be done, Carole was always glad to do it. She knew her friends could use help with the painting, but Carole just didn't feel ready to be with other people right then. She felt more like staying with the horses. She wondered where Red had disappeared to, but when she heard his voice in Max's office, she knew he would be particularly happy to have her help. Max and Red were having a loud conversation, making plans for the rest of the week. It seemed that The Saddle Club members weren't the only people who missed Mrs. Reg.

Without further hesitation Carole began her next job. One by one, she took the horses into the stalls. Each one had to be untacked, groomed, watered, and fed. Since it was evening and they wouldn't be going out of the stable again until morning, it had to be done right. Carole was good at this kind of work, but there weren't many shortcuts when it came to taking good care of horses. It was almost an hour before she could return to her friends. They would understand. At least she hoped they would.

When the last horse was groomed and fed and put up for the night, she was ready to go back to the painting. It was twilight. Carole hated to think about how much more work there would be to do. Three girls simply couldn't paint the entire front of stable in a few hours—even three very determined girls. They would have to work into the night and be at the stable even earlier the next morning. And then there would be tomorrow night. . . .

The thought alone exhausted Carole.

"Here I come," she announced to her friends as she walked toward the stable's front door. "Give me a brush. What needs to be done most?"

"Nothing," Lisa said as Carole emerged from the stable into the dim twilight. "It's all done."

"Very funny," Carole said.

"No joke," said Stevie.

Carole looked. The sky was darkening, but it wasn't so dark that she couldn't see the whole job had been finished. The front of the stable was now a beautiful deep red with a sparkling white trim. The job *was* done. The ladders, buckets, brushes, drop cloths, and hats were nowhere in sight.

"How could the two of you do all that work by yourselves?" Carole asked. She was totally astonished.

"We had some help," Lisa said.

"Santa's elves?" Carole asked. "It's not exactly the season, you know."

"No, more like the Jolly Green Giants—four of them in fact," Stevie said.

That could only mean one thing. "The basketball players?" she asked.

"You won't believe how high they could reach without even using a ladder!" Lisa said.

"You are amazing, Stevie. How did you talk those clowns into helping you?"

"I didn't have anything to do with it," Stevie said. "It was all you. When they saw how much work you were doing around here, they said that any place that inspired such devotion certainly deserved to have their help. They spent more than an hour doing all the hardest parts of the painting. Without them we'd be here until midnight. We have you to thank for their help."

"Me?" Carole asked. "I don't understand. They spent the whole day laughing at my silly mistakes."

"No," Lisa said. "They spent the whole day admiring what you were trying to do. They liked it so much, they want to sign up the whole rest of the basketball team for lessons. Max is going wild trying to figure out when he's going to fit them into the schedule, but Red is trying to talk him into buying some taller horses!"

Carole shook her head in disbelief. It was hard to imagine how so much good could come from one really dumb mistake. She was simply too tired to take it all in. It would have to wait for another day.

7

"ALL RIGHT, THEN, that's it," Stevie said—much more positively than she felt. "We all have our assignments, let's begin the day."

Carole snapped a salute at her and clicked her heels.

"Am I that bad?" Stevie asked sheepishly.

Lisa nodded.

Stevie was finding that when three girls were trying to equal one woman, it wasn't easy in more ways than one. It wasn't easy because it was hard to do the job, and it particularly wasn't easy because it was a strain on their friendship. Each of them was nervous that she was going to mess up and it would be her fault. There was so much to do and it was *so* important.

This morning, for example, Stevie had to figure out how to order food for the horses. She'd made the job sound light when she took it on, but the truth was, she wasn't at all sure about what to do, and she didn't want to goof.

Lisa's job could be even trickier. She'd volunteered to skip jump class to take the French ambassador out on a trail ride. The U.S. had pretty good relationships with France, and it seemed unlikely that anything Lisa would do, or not do, was going to change that. Still, it was a big responsibility.

Although Carole's job wouldn't affect international relations, or cost Pine Hollow a lot of money if she made a mistake, it was in its way even trickier than her friends' jobs. Carole had taken on the task of assigning horses to riders. She had already unfolded a giant chart she'd made last night to keep track of the names of riders and horses and class hours. She spread the chart out on Mrs. Reg's desk and looked pointedly at Stevie, who relinquished the chair. Carole instantly began scribbling on her chart. Lisa hurried to a quiet spot in the locker area and pulled out her French phrase book. Stevie headed for the feed shed.

She knew that feed for horses consisted primarily of hay and grain, both of which could be a fire hazard. She didn't exactly understand what caused spon-

taneous combustion in bales of hay, but she'd seen the
result in a barn fire once and never wanted to see it
again. Grain was a fire hazard because it was dusty and
the dust particles could almost hang in the air. In the
case of a fire—or even a spark that might start one—
the dust particles themselves would burn, and that
burning would be explosive. For those reasons most
stables, including Pine Hollow, stored their feed in a
separate shed. No matter how careful people were, ac-
cidents happened. Keeping the potential accident a
distance from the horses made the stable itself safer for
the animals.

Stevie opened the door to the feed shed and turned
on the light. Bags, barrels, and bales were piled neatly
everywhere. The place was pretty full, so it seemed
odd that Mrs. Reg wanted to order more for Friday,
but who was Stevie to disagree with something on
Mrs. Reg's list?

And who was Stevie to figure out what Mrs. Reg
wanted to order? And how on earth was she going to
do it?

She sat down on a bale of hay and began chewing on
a fingernail. It didn't taste very good, and it didn't
help her thinking. She stopped chewing on the nail
and looked around, hoping to pull an answer out of
thin air. And she did.

For there, fastened to a clipboard that was hanging from a hook by the door to the shed, was a piece of pink paper. On a hunch, Stevie walked over to look at it. It was an invoice, dated just a month earlier. At the top of the piece of paper, it gave the name of the place that had delivered the feed: Connor Hay & Grain. Then there was an address and a phone number. Better still, it said at the top: *Standing Order.* That meant that this was probably just about exactly what Mrs. Reg ordered every time she called.

"Bingo!" Stevie announced. She took the clipboard down off the hook and dashed back to Mrs. Reg's office, remembering to turn off the light and lock the door behind her. Maybe it wasn't so hard to be Mrs. Reg after all.

"BONJOUR," LISA SAID, practicing her welcome to the French ambassador. "*Je m'appelle Lisa Atwood.*" Introducing herself wouldn't be so hard. The hard part was going to be chatting about horseback riding, or international affairs—whatever the man wanted. She'd spent more than two hours the night before boning up on her horseback-riding vocabulary. She'd made herself a list, but she'd worked so hard on memorizing it that she hoped she wouldn't have to refer to it too much. Saddle, for instance, was *selle.* Sidesaddle was *selle d'amazone.* She didn't actually think she was going to need to talk about sidesaddles because she'd never even ridden one, but she was interested to learn that the name in French was connected with the women warriors, the Amazons. Perhaps she could work it into a conversation, although she didn't know the word for "warrior," and that would make it hard to talk about.

Lisa found that she did get mixed up between horses and hairs. In French the word for horse was *cheval* and more than one horse was *chevaux*. Hair, on the other hand, was *cheveux*. She certainly hoped she didn't goof and ask the poor ambassador if he wanted to ride any hairs!

A car pulled up to the stable. It was ten-fifteen. All the riders, plus Max and Red, were in the jump class. This could only be the French ambassador. When a distinguished-looking, middle-aged man stepped out of the car, Lisa knew she was right. She took a deep breath and went to work.

"*Bonjour,*" she began. "*Je m'appelle Lisa Atwood.*"

There was no question about it, the look on the man's face was complete surprise. Then he smiled. Lisa was terribly proud of herself.

"*Bonjour, Lisa,*" he said, offering his hand for a shake.

They had definitely gotten off on the right foot—or *pied*, as the French would say. Lisa began her carefully memorized words of welcome and explanation. She took the ambassador to the locker area and told him she would be putting *une selle* on his *cheval* and would meet him by the *porte d'ecurie en dix minutes*. That would give him ten minutes to get to the stable door. He said *merci beaucoup*, so Lisa figured that would be fine.

Quickly she tacked up Barq for herself and Delilah for the ambassador. Delilah was a beautiful palomino mare, and she was sure the man would be pleased to be able to ride her. Delilah was also very gentle, so no matter whether the ambassador was a good rider or not, Delilah would be a good horse for him.

The man was ready and waiting for Lisa when she appeared with his horse. Then came a tricky part. Pine Hollow's riders sometimes joked that the place was built on traditions, because it had an awful lot of them. One of the most important, however, was the good-luck horseshoe. Every rider was supposed to touch the horseshoe nailed up by the door before going out on a ride. No rider at Pine Hollow had ever been badly hurt, and tradition held that it was because of the horseshoe.

Lisa couldn't manage a long explanation, but she

could demonstrate. She mounted Barq, touched the shoe, and looked at the ambassador. *"Fer à cheval pour bonne chance,"* she said. He smiled at her and touched it as well. He'd understood! She was very pleased with herself. She felt as though she were riding on a new high as she led the way out the door and off to the trail through the field. She waved gaily at her jump classmates when they passed by.

"Au revoir," Stevie called. Lisa and the ambassador both shouted *"Au revoir"* back at her. That was French for good-bye, and it really meant "until we see one another again." That sounded so much nicer than "good-bye." Lisa found herself beginning to love the French language. That feeling made it much easier to speak in it, too. And as she spoke, she found that she lost some of her self-consciousness. Pretty soon she and her charge were chatting easily about various things that Lisa hadn't even known she knew how to say. She was, in fact, having fun, and so was the man who was riding with her.

She wanted to tell him about The Saddle Club. She had the feeling that this nice man would really understand. He was a good rider, and he was very friendly. Since those were the two basic requirements for membership, she wanted to explain it.

"Moi et mes amies," she began. *"Nous avons un,* uh,

une, oh, drat, *une* . . ." She groped for something that would be like the word "club" in French, but nothing came to her. "I just can't remember the word for 'club' in French," she said, and then shrugged sheepishly to convey to him that she was at a loss.

"I can't remember it, either," the man said. "But I suspect it's something like *club* or *associacion*. Anyway, why don't we try English for a while?"

It took Lisa about eight very long seconds to register what she'd just heard and what it really sounded like. In those eight seconds, she realized that she'd heard English spoken, and it wasn't accented English, unless you counted a pleasant southern Virginia drawl.

"You're not the French ambassador—you're not even French!" she stammered.

"Of course I am," the man said. "I'm Michael French. I thought you knew."

Mrs. Reg's list had said it was the French ambassador who was coming to ride. How could she have made a mistake like that? Then Lisa realized it wasn't Mrs. Reg who had made the mistake. It was The Saddle Club. Mrs. Reg had written "Thursday, 11, Am. French." She hadn't meant Am. French. She'd meant eleven A.M., and she'd just written it a little oddly.

Lisa wanted to disappear. Right then and there she wanted to find a way to be swallowed up by the earth. How could she have been so silly? There she'd been, speaking sort of pidgin French to this poor man, who really only wanted to ride a horse!

"Oh, no," she groaned. "I'm—" She couldn't even think of the words in English! "I can't—I mean, it's so—"

"Don't worry!" the man said. He actually sounded cheerful, which struck Lisa as odd. "I'm really very flattered," he went on. "See, I work for the government in the State Department. I would like nothing more than to be an ambassador. The fact that you thought I was one already—well, you can imagine, I've loved every minute of it. Besides, as you surely know, French is the language of diplomacy, and mine's been getting a little rusty, stuck in an office in Washington as I am. You gave me a chance to speak in French. It was terrific. I only expected to learn something about horseback riding. I got twice the value for my money!"

"You're being awfully nice about this," Lisa said, now not so eager to disappear into the earth. "In fact, I think you're giving me a lesson in diplomacy."

"Oh, but I mean it," Mr. French insisted. "And now

that we've brushed up my languages, let's see if you can do as well with the riding instruction, which I'm sure will be a little easier in our native tongue. Just exactly what was it you were trying to tell me about the Amazon River and women who ride horses?"

Lisa tried to stifle her giggle, but she couldn't contain it. "I guess I ride better than I speak French," she said when she could talk. "That has to do with side-saddles."

Much to Lisa's surprise and pleasure, Mr. French seemed genuinely interested in learning about side-saddles and everything else she could tell him about riding and horses. When they finally returned to Pine Hollow an hour and a half later, they'd had a great ride, and they'd both learned an awful lot. Mr. French had learned about horses. Lisa had learned about people.

"CAN YOU GET the order here by Friday?" Stevie asked. The man at the other end of the phone wasn't too happy with the question.

"We just delivered there. You need more already?"

"Look, I'm just filling in for Mrs. Reg," Stevie said. Although she usually felt that being devious was the way to accomplish something, in this case she suspected that straightforward begging was going to be the most effective. "She was called to the bedside of a very sick friend who needed her to nurse her, wipe her brow, feed her gruel—" Stevie wondered briefly what gruel was, but it sounded like something somebody who was sick would eat. "Selflessly she left her family and her home to be with her friend and asked that we do a few meager chores in her absence. Her thoughts were with those who needed her the most: her friend and the horses. Can we let them go without, just because Mrs. Reg—"

"All right, all right! Stop already!" the man practically hollered into the telephone. "You've got me crying, miss. We'll deliver. The stuff will be there Friday morning just like you asked. You may or may not have a future as a stable manager, but I'm sure you could get a job on a soap opera. . . ."

"Thanks for your help," Stevie said. "I know Mrs. Reg will be pleased and grateful and . . ."

"Yeah, and she'll wipe my brow and give me gruel when I get sick, huh?"

"I'll leave a note for her," Stevie said.

When they hung up, Stevie reflected on the conversation. Then she had a little laugh to herself, confident that in the office at Connor Hay & Grain there was a man who was doing exactly the same thing. The two of them had seen exactly eye to eye, and it had been fun.

Stevie sighed contentedly. Being a stable manager had its rewards.

8

CAROLE WAS VERY proud of her charts. It wasn't easy
to keep track of who was riding which horse when, but
it was important. For one thing, it was a way of keeping track of what riders were out. For another, and
really more important as far as Carole was concerned,
it was a way of telling how long each horse was working. Horses couldn't spend all day every day with riders
on their backs. Just like people, they needed time to
rest and recuperate. Mrs. Reg always tried to arrange it
so that no horse spent more than four hours a day in
class. Carole thought she could manage that, too.

Charts weren't all of the job, though. The harder
part was pleasing the riders. In Red's beginner class,

three of the girls had wanted to ride Delilah. Carole was almost relieved when she saw that Lisa had taken the mare for the French ambassador. That way the girls couldn't fight over her. Instead they began fighting about which one of them was going to ride Patch. Carole solved that problem by talking louder than the squabbling young riders. She put them each on horses they hadn't ridden before and told each—in a whisper—that they were getting the best horse. That at least worked.

Now in a quiet moment (because all the squabbling little girls were in class with Red), Carole turned to her other job for the day, which was to look for the pin some more, though she was becoming more and more certain they would not be able to find it. Carole decided it was time to make a careful examination of the stable area, particularly the wide aisle that ran between the stalls in the U-shaped stable. There was always a layer of straw on the floor there, and that was just the sort of camouflage a gold pin could use to hide out.

Carole picked up a pitchfork and began working on the straw methodically. She picked up a forkful and shook it, hoping to find a gold pin dropping out of the mass of straw. Then, when nothing gold fell out, she put down that forkful and picked up another. By the time she'd picked up eight forkfuls, she'd decided it was almost impossible that this would work. Still, she didn't have a better idea. She picked up her ninth forkful. Then her tenth and her eleventh . . .

"Don't look at me that way," she said to Starlight, who was gazing at her curiously over the door to his stall. Starlight didn't have anything to say to that. He pulled his head back in. Carole continued her work in silence.

Most of the horses were now out on trail rides or busy in classes. The stable was unusually quiet, and Carole was hopeful that it would make it easier for her to hear the very welcome *thump* of a solid gold pin hitting the wide boards of the stable floor. No matter how much she listened, though, there was no such *thump*.

There was, however, another sound, and it was coming from the tack room. Carole stopped her work and listened. Then she was sure. There was definitely some sniffling going on. It didn't sound like an allergy or a cold, either. It sounded very unhappy.

Carole propped the pitchfork up against a beam and peered into the tack room. Somebody was in there crying and probably wanted to be alone. Carole didn't intend to interrupt unless she seemed to be needed.

One look and Carole knew she was needed. There

sat May Grover, one of Pine Hollow's young riders and a particular favorite of Carole's. May was crying her eyes out.

"Could you use a friend?" Carole asked.

"I don't have any," May said, tears streaming down her face, but the look in her eyes said that, more than anything, she wanted Carole to come be with her.

Carole came in and perched on the bench next to May. She reached into her jeans pocket and found a tissue. Silently she offered it to the young girl. While May blew her nose, Carole recalled a conversation she'd overheard earlier between May and her friend Jessica. Before class May had been telling the other young rider in no uncertain terms just exactly how to do something, and Jessica hadn't reacted kindly. Carole thought she recalled, in fact, that Jessica had told May just exactly what to do with the rest of her life. It hadn't been nice, but even best friends had arguments sometimes. Carole hadn't taken it very seriously. May apparently had.

May was wise and strong. At least that was how she always appeared. As a result, her classmates sometimes thought she was a little bossy. She knew an awful lot about horses and tended to lecture her friends. Being right wasn't always enough. That was something

Carole had learned long ago, and she had the feeling that it was May's turn to learn it now.

"Is it what Jessica said?" Carole asked May.

May looked at Carole in surprise, totally unaware of the fact that Carole had heard the argument. Carole had a funny feeling then. There was one person who always seemed to be aware of what was going on among the young riders, even when they had no idea that she was aware of it at all, and that was Mrs. Reg. Now Carole and her friends were trying, in their own way, to replace Mrs. Reg, and Carole was finding that she was replacing her in more than one way. In her absence Carole was somehow becoming a person who knew what was going on.

What would Mrs. Reg do if she were here, Carole wondered. In the first place, she wouldn't let on that she knew what had happened. In the second place, she'd tell a story. Mrs. Reg had a story for every occasion. It was her way of telling the riders that she knew what was happening and of offering advice very indirectly. In fact, sometimes she was so indirect that it took the riders days to figure out what she was saying. They all enjoyed the challenge of untangling a tale Mrs. Reg had spun. But Mrs. Reg wasn't here to spin the tale. On the other hand, Carole was.

"There was a horse here once," Carole began, not having the faintest idea where she was going. Mrs. Reg almost always started her stories that way, though, and Carole trusted she'd get some inspiration. "He was a feisty one, that horse." Nice start, Carole told herself. May was feisty, too. Surely she'd be able to come up with something for May.

"He used to like to play in the pasture all the time." Carole could visualize this made-up pony, and she began to describe him for May. He was a bay with three white socks and a white blaze. His coat was a rich reddish-brown. He had a very smooth, supple walk, and he was the best jumper in the stable. That was a nice touch because May loved to jump horses.

Carole's story took on a life of its own. She added a mare who was the bay's best friend, and they would spend their summer days in the field, prancing and playing in the sunshine. And when little boys and girls wanted to ride them, the two of them just loved it. They liked being friends with the boys and girls best of all—much better than with the grown-ups at the stable. But then one day, the mare was sold and the bay became terribly lonely. He wouldn't eat the sweet grass in the field, and he lost a lot of weight. He even found he didn't like the children so much. Until one day a new horse came to the stable, and he became friends with the new horse.

Carole stopped her story there. She thought that was probably enough and that May would be comforted by the story as it stood. As it was with Mrs. Reg's stories, May was going to have to do a little thinking about what, exactly, the story meant.

May didn't have to do any thinking at all. She decided right away. She gave Carole a great big hug.

"Oh, Carole, I'm so sorry! But it's going to be better soon. Don't you worry."

She handed Carole the tissue she'd been using. She picked up her hard hat and thrust it on her head, snapping the strap efficiently.

"See you later!" she said. "And I want there to be a smile on your face next time, too!"

In an instant she was gone, leaving Carole alone with her thoughts. All of them revolved around what on earth May had made of the story she'd told. She'd obviously completely missed the point about how a new friend would come into her life. Somehow May had decided the story had to do with Carole, and she seemed to feel terribly sorry for Carole.

So much for trying to be Mrs. Reg. Instead of comforting May and giving her some understanding of what had happened between herself and Jessica, Carole's story had ended with May trying to comfort Carole. Carole scratched her head. The world didn't seem to be in working order at all.

On the other hand, something good had happened. May had been crying when Carole found her in the tack room. She'd been smiling by the time she'd left. It seemed that May had quite missed the point of Carole's story, but she hadn't been able to evade Carole's purpose—that being to cheer her up. Carole smiled to herself. Maybe it wasn't just exactly the way Mrs. Reg would have done it, but whatever it was she'd done, it had worked.

Carole made a mental note to herself to ask Mrs. Reg when she got back what she would have done. Then she changed her mind about it. She knew just what Mrs. Reg would do: She'd tell *Carole* a story about a horse at Pine Hollow, and then Carole would have to figure out what that was about. No, she decided, I'll just let this whole episode pass.

9

IT WAS TIME for Carole to get back to her charts. There, at least, she was confident. She could assign horses to riders, noting what she'd done, and everything would be right there in front of her. She headed for Mrs. Reg's office, hoping this job would give her more satisfaction and success than a few of her more recent tasks.

The young riders who were involved in the summer-camp program each had their horses assigned for the day. That took care of that. However, some of them came in only part-time, so their horses were now available for the noontime adult class. It took Carole a few minutes to sort out exactly what horses were available, and when she looked up from her chart, she found herself surrounded by six adult riders, all appearing to be none too patient.

"Can I get my horse now?" one woman asked testily.

"Of course," Carole said. She smiled diplomatically at the woman.

"I want the same one I rode last week," the woman said.

"And that was . . . ?" Carole asked.

"I can't remember its name, but it was brown," the woman informed Carole. This wasn't very informative, however, since ninety percent of the horses at the stable were one shade or another of brown. All she'd eliminated, really, were Pepper, a dappled gray who had been retired to the pasture; Delilah, the palomino; and Patch, the piebald.

"Bay or chestnut?" Carole asked, trying to narrow the field further.

"What's the difference?"

This wasn't going to be easy. Patiently Carole explained to the woman that bays were brown with black tails and manes. Chestnuts were solid shades of brown, often reddish, sometimes almost a golden color.

It took a few minutes, but they finally narrowed down the selection, and Carole assigned a horse to the woman. She *thought* it was the same horse the woman

had ridden the week before, but she was quite confident that even if it wasn't, the woman would never
know the difference.

"Next?"

"I want a different horse from the last one I rode in
class," the next rider said. She smiled thinly at Carole,
suggesting she didn't mean the smile at all. "I had a lot
of trouble with him, and I don't want to spend the
class time training *your* horse how to ride."

Carole didn't like the sound of this. All horses could
be troublesome from time to time, but the Pine Hollow horses were really well trained. She knew from
experience that when horses misbehaved, usually it
was the rider's fault, not the horse's. Horses were naturally competitive, including competition with their
riders. If a rider didn't establish who was in charge
from the moment she got into the saddle, she was
going to spend most of her time up there arguing with
the horse about who was the boss. This woman who
had wasted no time in establishing that she was going
to be in charge of Carole's decision-making had apparently been unable to do the same with a horse.

"Who did you ride last time?" Carole asked.

"Barq," the woman answered.

That was a surprise. Barq was a really good horse.
He could be a handul, but he certainly wasn't moody.

Carole started to wonder what the woman had done to get off on the wrong foot with Barq, but then realized that wasn't going to be productive. Her job was simply to give her a horse she would get along with.

"Now, don't give me some old nag," the woman said. "I had one of those once, and I spent the entire class kicking the old boy to get him to keep up with everybody else."

That would have been Pepper, Carole thought. Pepper didn't much like to be kicked. It would have made him go slower, too. This woman wasn't having any luck at all.

"So give me a horse with some spirit that I won't have trouble controlling. I've spoken with Max about my problems in this regard," the woman said. "I just don't intend to spend a lot of time riding at this stable if I can't get a decent mount. There *are* other stables around here, you know."

Carole didn't like the sound of this, and she didn't feel comfortable being on the spot. She and her friends were trying to help Max and Mrs. Reg. If she made a mistake here and cost Pine Hollow a rider, that would hardly be considered helpful.

"So what are you going to do?" the woman demanded.

Carole had no idea. "I think we can solve your problem," she said, stalling because she didn't know what she was going to do. What this woman wanted was a perfect horse that didn't require a perfect rider. She wanted a horse who was gentle and obedient, but who had spirit and was fun to ride. As far as Carole was concerned, that was a perfect description of only one horse—her own Starlight. It would mean she would miss a class, but she probably would have to do that anyway. Carole picked up the pencil, pleased with her solution to the problem. She was about to write in "Starlight" next to the woman's name, but she realized that wasn't a solution at all. For one thing, it was strictly against the rules to assign private horses to class riders—even her own horse. For another, it just wasn't right. All of the horses at Pine Hollow were good horses, and if she assigned Starlight to this woman, she'd be saying that wasn't so.

The woman cleared her throat impatiently.

"I think I have just the horse for you," Carole said, mentally running through all the horses on the list to figure out what horse she'd give to the woman. Then she saw the answer.

"His name is Patch. He's a piebald."

"Piebald? You mean like a pinto? A Western horse?" She said the words with disdain.

Carole could hardly believe her ears. Even the

greenest rider should be aware of the fact that the color or markings of a horse had absolutely nothing to do with the quality of a horse. It should be the last consideration when choosing a horse. This woman was definitely difficult! Then Carole found the solution.

"Did you know that Velvet's horse in *National Velvet* was a piebald?" Carole asked. "That's why she called him Pie."

"Really?" the woman asked. "The horse that won the race?" Carole nodded. The woman smiled then, and it seemed genuine. Carole had found the key. She wrote "Patch" next to the woman's name and made a note on Patch's section of the chart.

"Next?" Carole said.

The rest of the class turned out to be easier, and Carole was relieved. Assigning horses was a much bigger task than she'd ever thought. When the last of the lunchtime class was assigned, Carole sat back in Mrs. Reg's chair and put her feet on the desk. She deserved a little relaxation as a reward for her brilliant piece of diplomacy.

Her eyes lit on Mrs. Reg's infamous list. What more was there for the girls to do? Then Carole spotted Mr. Jarvis's name on the list. She looked at her watch. He was due at one o'clock, so that meant he'd be here any minute. Carole put her feet back down on the floor. She'd been telling herself all morning that she had to ask Max or Red just exactly what horse it was that Mr. Jarvis wanted. Now he'd be here in a minute, and she had no idea. Then she reminded herself that she'd just negotiated a very tricky settlement with a very fussy rider. If she could make that woman happy, she could surely make Mr. Jarvis happy.

A car pulled up. That had to be Mr. Jarvis. He was the only rider expected at this time. A few minutes later, Mr. Jarvis entered Mrs. Reg's office. He was surprised to see Carole at the desk.

"Mrs. Reg, you've shrunk!" he teased.

Carole immediately liked the man. She grinned and offered her hand. "I'm Carole Hanson," she said. "Mrs. Reg is away for a couple of days, and my friends and I are trying to replace her, though of course that's not an easy job. Anyway, you must be Mr. Jarvis. Mrs. Reg left us very specific instructions about you, sir, and said we had to have the right horse for you."

Carole was adopting the theory that the less sure she was about something, the more important it was to *sound* sure.

"Well then, she told you about me and Patch, didn't she?"

"Patch?"

"He's the only horse at Pine Hollow that I'll ever ride."

"Patch?"

This wasn't going well.

"She probably didn't tell you why, but it's an old story. I won't bore you with it—"

"Oh, I wouldn't be bored," Carole said, thinking that as long as the man was talking, she wouldn't have to tell him about the woman in the lunchtime class who was already riding Patch and who would now never give him up.

"It has to do with pintos," the man said. "The first horse I ever rode was a pinto, and I decided then that I always wanted to ride them. I know a horse's color has nothing to do with his quality"—and that put him a few steps above the woman who was now riding Patch—"but I'm very superstitious, and I simply can't be on anything but a pinto."

"Interesting," Carole said, though "interesting" wasn't what she was actually thinking. "Bad news" was more like it. She stalled.

"Also," the man went on, "I'm an artist. I paint with oils. It seems only right that a painter should ride painted ponies, don't you think?"

"Absolutely," Carole said. "It makes complete sense

to me." It didn't make any sense at all. By that same logic, since she was still in school, she should want to ride only horses who hadn't finished their schooling! Still Mr. Jarvis was apparently a good customer. Carole wanted to keep him happy. Then a thought occurred to her. Maybe, just maybe.

She scratched her head thoughtfully and considered the idea that had popped into her head. It was a Stevie Lake idea, if there ever had been one, and it was a gamble, but it seemed the only possibility. Carole wanted to please this nice, if slightly strange, man. Perhaps she could do it.

"I have to tell you that Patch is being ridden now," Carole said.

The man began to say something that Carole didn't think she wanted to hear, so she went on talking herself.

"Patch may be our only pinto, but he's not the only horse here that you will like. You go change into your riding clothes and wait for me by the door. Let me tack up another horse for you. I'll bring him to the good-luck horseshoe, and we'll meet you there."

"I only ride pintos!" the man said.

"I know," Carole said. "I know. And I think you'll find this one quite satisfactory."

Without further ado, she rose from the desk and

went to the stalls, sending Mr. Jarvis to the locker area.

Carole picked up some tack and went to the horse she'd assigned to Mr. Jarvis. "Piebald" was one of the English terms for black-and-white-patched horses, and "skewbald" horses had brown patches instead of black. In Spanish both of these were known as "pintos." Another English name for a pinto was "paint" or "painted horse." Now Pine Hollow had only one pinto, but as of the previous afternoon, they did have another painted horse. The colors weren't black and white—they were red and white.

"Hi there, Diablo," Carole said, patting him affectionately. She gave him a carrot, too, just to show that there were no hard feelings about the little chase they'd had in the field. He didn't seem to be harboring any grudges.

Carole inspected the paint job. She and Stevie and Lisa had been working at it quite unsuccessfully. It was going to take a lot of brushing to get it all out. Eventually the hairs would grow out and Diablo would be his same old dark brown, but for now, and for some time to come, he was decidedly brown, red, and white.

She tacked him up and led him to the door of the stable, where she found Mr. Jarvis waiting.

"I only—"

"It's a paint," she said, cutting off his words of protest. "I promise. And he's a terrific horse."

When she drew up to him, she made sure that she walked Diablo far enough into the sunlight for his very special red and white markings to be distinctly visible.

Mr. Jarvis looked. Then he looked again. He was about to speak, but he stopped himself. Carole held her tongue. That's just what Stevie would have done.

"Well, I never—" Mr. Jarvis said. But he wasn't angry, he was smiling. Then he laughed. "I guess if there's more than one way to skin a cat, there's got to be more than one way to paint a horse! All right. You win. I'll try this fellow. What's his name?"

"Diablo," Carole said. "He's a great horse, but be nice to him. He had kind of a rough day yesterday."

"At the beauty parlor?" Mr. Jarvis joked.

"Sort of," Carole conceded.

Mr. Jarvis took the reins from Carole and mounted Diablo. He brushed the good-luck horseshoe with his hand. He sat pensively in the saddle for a few minutes, trying to get the feel of the horse beneath him. He leaned forward and patted Diablo's neck. Then he turned to Carole.

"I noticed the new paint job on the front of the

stable as I came in," he said. "I told myself it was nice of you to paint the place just for me. I didn't realize at the time how true that was."

Carole saluted him in her best Marine Corps style. "We always try to please our customers, *sir*," she said.

"I can tell," he said. Then he signaled Diablo to head for the trails. Off they went, painter and painted pony together.

10

"IF ONE MORE person tells me that they want a gentle horse with some spirit, I think I'm going to scream," Carole said to her friends when they were all safely hidden in the hayloft above the stalls at Pine Hollow. They were having an impromptu Saddle Club meeting. They really needed one another.

"I can't tell you how awful it was to learn that only the man's *name* was French! He was as American as I am—as we all are—and he spoke pretty good French, too. Can you imagine? I thought he was the ambassador!" Lisa found herself reliving her profound embarrassment when she realized the mistake she and her friends had made.

"Do you think it was my fault?" Stevie asked defensively. "I mean, that's what Mrs. Reg's list said."

"I truly wish I could blame you for it," Lisa said. "But the fact is, I saw the list just like you did, and I drew exactly the same conclusion you did. We both got to thinking about Estelle and the Brazilian ambassador. No, I don't blame you."

Carole snapped the pop top of a can of soda and took a long drink. It tasted awfully good on the dusty warm afternoon. Lisa sipped at her apple juice. Stevie just stared blankly at the soda can in her hand. She was thinking hard.

"You know who we could really use at a time like this?" she asked.

Lisa nodded. "Sure, Mrs. Reg. She'd have a story for us about how some horses tried to band together when a friend of theirs left."

"No, maybe it would be about how Max—*her* Max—tried to fill in for the county doctor when he went on vacation," Stevie suggested.

"Or about how the farrier's wife learned to shoe horses just because her husband sprained his knee in the three-legged race at the church social and couldn't hold a horse's hoof between his knees long enough to shoe it," Carole said.

Lisa liked that one. She began laughing a little. It

was the first time she'd laughed all day, and it felt
pretty good. Mrs. Reg's stories were always more than a
little offbeat, and sometimes the girls suspected that
they weren't based on the absolute truth. It didn't take
away from their charm, because they knew that there
was always something to learn from them. Right now
it seemed that the one thing one of Mrs. Reg's stories
could do for them would be to provide a good laugh.

Suddenly Lisa had a mental image of the farrier,
complete with his leather apron, running a three-
legged race. The image was absurd and it tickled her
funny bone.

That was when Lisa's shoulders started shaking with
laughter. Then while her friends watched, her giggles
exploded, and they were positively infectious. Within
a matter of seconds, Carole and Stevie joined in.
None of it made any sense at all, and all of it seemed
like the funniest thing that any one of the three of
them had ever thought about. They laughed until the
tears came, and then they laughed some more—until
the tears rolled down their cheeks.

Each, in a corner of her heart and her mind, understood what was happening. The three of them had
taken on an enormous amount of worry and work
when they'd offered to do Mrs. Reg's job, and it
seemed that everything they tried to do came out all

wrong: a humongous paint job they couldn't possibly finish themselves, culminating in paint splattered on Diablo; saddling up ponies for six-foot-tall men; French lessons for an American rider; and at the bottom of it all, there was still no sign of Mrs. Reg's pin. The perfect antidote for such an exhausting and nerve-racking week was being together and acting silly.

Finally the laughter began to subside, but not the wonderful feeling of warmth and friendship it had brought. The girls understood, without saying anything among themselves, that the most valuable thing they had—more valuable even than a solid-gold pin with a diamond—was the love and friendship they had for one another.

"I just had a thought," Carole said when she could finally speak. Lisa and Stevie looked at her. "I was thinking about Mrs. Reg and what she would say if she could see us right now."

"That's easy," Stevie said.

Lisa painted a stern Mrs. Reg look on her face (although Mrs. Reg rarely looked stern), lowered her voice, and spoke the words for the absent woman, "What are you girls laughing about? Isn't there work to be done around here? You think this is some kind of game parlor?"

Since that was just about exactly what Mrs. Reg

would have said, all three girls began laughing again. But they didn't laugh as hard this time. The mention of Mrs. Reg reminded them what the underlying problem was. In the first place, they weren't doing her job very well. In the second place, but it was really the first place, they still hadn't found the pin.

"Oh, right," Stevie said, suddenly very sober.

"This was fun, but you know, I think we're really mess-ups," Lisa said. "I mean, every time I think about that poor Mr. French, I just can't believe what I did."

"*We* did, you mean," Stevie said generously. "But don't take it so hard, Lisa. After all, the guy thought it was funny, and he seemed to have a wonderful time. He *did* make an appointment to come back again next week."

"You're right," Lisa said. "But when he made the next appointment, he made me schedule it for Mr. English."

"See, he has a sense of humor," Carole said. "That's more than I can say for those basketball players."

"What are you saying?" Stevie asked. "They *loved* you."

"Sure, because they think I'm a complete ditz."

"Who cares?" Lisa asked. "I mean, I know they hurt your feelings, but you must have also impressed them. They pitched in and helped with the painting. We never would have finished if it hadn't been for them."

"I guess if it hadn't been for the painting, we never would have had a horse for Mr. Jarvis to ride, would we?" Carole said slowly.

"It seems that there's a pattern emerging here," Stevie said philosophically. She wasn't usually philosophical, so her friends listened carefully. "On the surface of it, we appear to be messing up totally, but when you look a little closer, it seems to be working for the best."

Lisa thought about that for a moment. Stevie was right, but she had the nagging feeling that doing things right in the first place was easier than messing up and then trying to find the silver lining to the cloud.

"You have a point," she finally conceded. "On the other hand, there's always tomorrow."

"Like what do you mean?" Carole asked.

"Well, we have until five o'clock tomorrow afternoon when Mrs. Reg is due back. Just think of all the things we could mess up before then. . . ."

"No, don't," Stevie countered. "Think of all the things we can make go right before then."

"Think of all the gold pins we can find before she gets back," Carole said.

Lisa looked at her watch. They had twenty-three and a half hours until Mrs. Reg's return. Considering what they'd done with the previous seventy-two hours, she wasn't very hopeful. She didn't share that thought with her friends. She didn't have to. The looks on their faces said they'd had the same thought all on their own.

11

On Friday morning Stevie sat at Mrs. Reg's desk and tugged at some of her hair. During these days when she and her friends had been trying to fill Mrs. Reg's shoes, Stevie had often found herself tugging at her hair. It didn't help much, but it was better than gritting her teeth. Her hair would grow back.

"But he *did* the wrong thing!" a very unpleasant voice whined at Stevie.

The voice belonged to none other than Veronica diAngelo, and the fact that it was unpleasant was nothing new. The fact that it was whining at her wasn't particularly new either, but the fact that she was supposed to do something about it *was* new, and Stevie didn't much like it.

The problem had to do with Garnet's grain ration. Most of the horses at Pine Hollow got the same feed for every meal all the time. Most horses had special diets some of the time, and a few had special diets all of the time. Pine Hollow could certainly manage that. There was a big chart in the feed shed, not far from the clipboard where Stevie had found the papers for the feed order, that showed who was supposed to eat what. Garnet had been put on a special diet. She was supposed to get a mixture of bran and whole oats in the morning for a week, while most of the other horses in the stable simply got crimped oats.

"There wasn't any bran in her feed this morning, and I could see that the oats in her bucket were crimped and not whole. Once again, Red has made a *terrible* mistake."

Red was standing next to Veronica. Right then his face was bright red with anger—even redder than his hair. He wasn't saying anything, though. He'd learned long ago not to argue with Veronica. She was just too dangerous. So it was up to Stevie to solve the problem.

It was a problem, too. Red *had* made a mistake. Veronica's horse wasn't supposed to get crimped oats because Veronica's father paid extra for her to have whole oats. Also, Judy Barker, the vet, had advised them to add the bran to Garnet's feed as a mild laxative because Veronica had been complaining that the horse had seemed sluggish. Garnet wasn't in any way *sick*, so Red's mistake was just that—a little goof—one that could easily be corrected with the horse's evening meal. However, Veronica seemed determined to make a federal case out of it.

"Judy *prescribed* this special diet for my horse, you know. It's not just that I think it would be nice for Garnet to get something special. It's been *prescribed* by a *doctor.*"

Stevie was fully aware of the fact that Judy was a doctor, and she didn't need Veronica to spit the words at her. In fact, she didn't think she needed Veronica at all. She wished she had the power to tell Veronica exactly what she was thinking, but she didn't. Veronica was a paying customer of Pine Hollow and deserved to get what she paid for.

Stevie looked at Red for help, but she could tell she wasn't going to get any. Red was holding his breath to keep from saying what was on his mind, and it wasn't an apology. Stevie thought Veronica deserved an apology. She also thought she deserved something else, and she suddenly had an idea of how she was going to deliver it to her.

"Well, Red," Stevie said finally. "It looks like we have made a little mistake here. . . ."

"*Little!*" Veronica sputtered, but Stevie continued talking before Veronica could start in again.

". . . and we're just going to have to make apologies and amends."

Those were the words Veronica was waiting to hear, and in her usual thoughtful and kind way, she told Stevie so.

"And just exactly how do you propose to do that?" she demanded.

Stevie pasted an angelic smile on her face. "Well, we're going to give Garnet the correct feed right now. Red?"

"Now?" he asked. "But Ste—"

"Now," Stevie said. She tried to sound authoritative without being bossy. It wasn't easy. She hoped she was managing it. Red didn't seem to think so. He tried again.

"I don't think—"

"We ought to correct this goof immediately," Stevie said calmly. "We wouldn't want Garnet to go without her bran and her whole oats, would we?"

"I could, but . . ."

"I know you're busy, Red," Stevie said sympathetically. "However, Veronica is right, and we just can't waste a second. We have to make it up to her. Right away."

Red got it. "You're absolutely right, Stevie. I'll get right on it."

"Thank you," Veronica said in a superior tone, "it's about time you took me seriously." She turned on her heel and stormed out of the office.

When they were pretty sure she was out of sight and earshot, Red offered his hand to Stevie for a high five. "I'm out of here," he said. "I've got work to do!"

Stevie grinned to herself. She'd accomplished something really good, and she felt good about it. Red was going to feed Garnet another full ration of grains, including the bran. The horse really didn't need the additional feeding, but it wouldn't harm him. It would, however, harm Veronica. There was no way she would be allowed to ride Garnet right after the horse had his ration of grain. It was a bad practice to ride a horse hard on a stomach filled with rich grains. So what Stevie had accomplished through the back door was something she never could have done in any direct way—she'd gotten Veronica out of jump class for the morning. It was just for an hour, but an hour without Veronica was a whole lot better than an hour with Veronica.

Satisfied with her own cleverness, she sat back in Mrs. Reg's chair, propped her feet on Mrs. Reg's desk, and grinned to herself.

"You look like the cat that ate the canary," Carole commented, walking into the office. She brushed Stevie's feet off the desk and laid out her new daily horse-assignment chart. "Tell me what's going on."

Stevie did. Carole loved it. She especially liked the part that a nice horse like Garnet would be getting a double treat—two rations of grain and the opportunity to miss a class with Veronica.

"Can't tell who's getting the better end of this deal, can we?" Carole asked.

Stevie was so proud of what she'd done that she wished there were more time to gloat. However, class was about to begin, and Mrs. Reg's office flooded with young riders, each clamoring for his or her favorite horse or pony. Carole was suddenly totally immersed in horse assignments.

"Oh, Stevie!" It was Lisa, calling from the front of the stable. Stevie was glad because that meant she had somebody else to tell about her victory over Veronica. It probably also meant that the delivery of hay and grain from Connor's was arriving. She grabbed the invoice from the last order just so she could check what was being delivered. She left the desk and the horse assignments to Carole and went to join her friend out in front of the stable.

"Stevie!" There was an urgency in Lisa's voice that

made Stevie quicken her step, though she wasn't really worried—because what could possibly ruin a morning in which she'd so totally outmaneuvered Veronica diAngelo?

When she stepped out the door of the stable, the answer to the question was right in front of her nose. It was an eighteen-wheel semi with large letters proclaiming it to be from Connor Hay & Grain.

The driver leaned out the window. "Where does Mrs. Reg want me to put all this stuff?" he asked.

"In the feed shed, like usual," Stevie said.

"This doesn't fit in the feed shed like usual," the man said. "This is a big order."

Stevie and Lisa looked at the truck. It was big. Really big. Stevie had seen deliveries from Connor's before. They usually just brought a few bags of grain and a couple hundred pounds of hay in the back of a pickup truck. They never brought it in a big truck like this—except for once when there was a three-day event at Pine Hollow and more than five times the usual number of horses were staying at the stable in temporary stalls.

Stevie tugged at her hair because as sure as Veronica diAngelo was going to have to stay out of jump class, Stevie knew that she'd done something wrong ordering the feed. But what?

Then a thought began forming in her mind. She hadn't looked at the date on the invoice before. She pulled the sheet of paper from her pocket and looked at it.

"Girls, why don't you go get Mrs. Reg so she can tell us what to do?" the driver asked. He was getting a little annoyed at Stevie, but not anywhere near as annoyed as Stevie was getting at herself.

There was the answer in black and white. The order she'd so happily duplicated had been placed exactly one week before the horse show at Pine Hollow. What she had sitting in the driveway was enough grain, hay, and straw to feed and bed hundreds of horses—not just the ones who lived at Pine Hollow, but ones from all over the county and then some.

It occurred to Stevie that perhaps the whole truckload wasn't for Pine Hollow. The stable had been doing business with Connor's for generations. Connor's certainly knew how much food they delivered regularly and that this "standing order" was intended to apply only to the annual horse show. Stevie felt silly having thought that the worst had happened.

"This whole truckload isn't for us, right?" Stevie asked confidently.

"Every bit of it," the man answered. "Just like you ordered. Now would you please go get Mrs. Reg?"

The worst had happened.

"I'll see what I can do," Stevie said weakly. She grabbed Lisa's sleeve and pulled her with her toward the office.

"What's going on?" Lisa asked.

It was hard to admit what a gigantic mistake she'd made, but Stevie explained it to Lisa, and when she did, Lisa groaned. "Oh, no."

"Oh, yes."

"But why don't you just tell them we don't need it?"

"I ordered it; I begged them for it," Stevie said.

"But we can't keep an order that size. There's no place to store it, and it will go bad."

Lisa was right about that. Fresh hay and grain were important. Horse feed that sat around was likely to become moldy, and moldy feed led to sick horses. She didn't have any idea what they were going to do, but the answer was not going to be to keep the whole order.

Stevie didn't even bother sitting at Mrs. Reg's desk. She just picked up the phone and dialed the number on the invoice.

She recognized the voice of the man she'd talked to earlier in the week. "Hi, I'm calling from Pine Hollow," she began.

"Oh, it's you," the man said. He sighed. Stevie wondered what that meant. "Listen, I'm glad you called. I got to ask you something really important."

Stevie was preparing herself to explain about her awful goof. She was so busy doing that in her mind that she almost missed what he was saying.

". . . Look, I'm sorry to ask you to do this, but there's an emergency over at the racetrack."

"What?" Stevie asked.

"I said, they had a fire in their grain shed at the racetrack. Everything is gone. The whole barn just blew up. And there's a meet going on. They've got a couple hundred horses over there, and they all need feed and grain. I'm asking all the stable owners around if they can cut back on their orders for right now so that we can supply the racetrack. I mean, if I don't get a truckload of feed over to them today . . . I know you need this order, but could you consider just taking partial delivery—for now? Please?" His words hung in the air. Stevie was stunned. She dropped into the chair at Mrs. Reg's desk, apparently completely unaware of the fact that she was sitting on Carole's lap.

"You mean, like you just want us to take a small portion of this gigantic delivery?" Stevie asked.

"If you possibly could," the man said. He sounded as

if he were pleading with her. In fact, it sounded like the kind of pleading Stevie had been about to do herself. It sounded more beautiful than a whole choir of angels!

This was the kind of situation Stevie liked best. It was a victory when she had absolutely no reason to expect one. It was as sweet as could be, and she was tempted to permit the poor man to beg some more. She couldn't do it, though. One reason she couldn't do it was that it wasn't fair to the man, who was just trying to do what was right for the horses at the racetrack. Another reason she couldn't do it was that she was about to start laughing, very hard.

"This is your lucky day," she said. "And mine, too."

"It is?"

"Yes," she assured the man. And then she explained. She told him about how she had just been guessing about what they needed, and when she'd found the old invoice, she hadn't even noticed that it was for the time they'd had the horse show. In fact, she explained, it seemed to her that there still was plenty of grain and hay in the feed shed, but since Mrs. Reg had wanted to have food by Friday, she thought they ought to take something. Could they have the amount they usually ordered—not for the horse show—and then could Connor's send the whole rest of the order to the racetrack?

"All the rest?" the man asked. "You sure you don't need it?"

"Every bit of it," Stevie said. "We don't even have a place to store it."

"You're right, this is my lucky day. I cleaned out my stores to fill your order because of all that funny stuff you said about Mrs. Reg and her sick friend—you know, the line about feeding her gruel. Now I find that when I'm in trouble, you guys come through for me just like Mrs. Reg does for her best friend."

"You want me to give you some gruel?" Stevie asked.

"No thanks," he said. "A truckload of grain and hay will do very nicely. Let me talk to the driver, okay?"

It was all settled in a matter of minutes. The driver and his assistant unloaded a very small portion of what was on the very big truck and headed for the racetrack with all the rest.

"Whew!" was all Stevie could say as she watched the truck drive away.

"Time for jump class," Carole reminded her.

"Ah, without Veronica," Stevie said. Maybe this day wasn't going to be so bad after all.

THREE O'CLOCK, FRIDAY. Normally Lisa was upset when it was three o'clock on Friday because on the summer schedule it meant that the week of riding was over and it was time for the weekend with no classes. Today she was sorry that the classes were finished, but she was really sorry that Mrs. Reg would be back in two hours and there was still no sign of her pin. The beautiful solid-gold, diamond-eyed horse was lost forever.

It was hard for Lisa to tell what upset her about it the most—the fact that she was responsible, the fact that the pin was valuable, or the fact that the pin had been a very special present to Mrs. Reg from her husband, who had died a long time ago. She'd thought about little else but the pin for days, and she hadn't been able to answer that question. What it came down to was that the pin was gone, and Mrs. Reg was going to be very sad, angry, and upset. Maybe there would even be some kind of punishment—like banning Lisa and her friends from riding at Pine Hollow. If that happened, Lisa couldn't blame Mrs. Reg in the least. She could only blame herself.

The riders walked their horses in a circle to cool them down, and as they passed Red, who stood by the edge of the ring, they pulled whips out of a bucket. One of them had a soda cap on the end, and the rider who got that whip was responsible for bringing cool drinks to everybody else while they untacked their horses. Carole got the soda whip. Lisa signaled to her that she'd be more than willing to untack Starlight while Carole took care of her task.

"Thanks, but let Stevie do it," Carole said, "You're going to want to spend some extra time on Diablo's grooming."

Lisa had forgotten. The advantage to riding Diablo was that when you were in the saddle, you couldn't see all the paint that was still on his rear. Lisa had been reminded of it, however, each time she'd passed Max in classes all day long, because he made an odd face every time he saw it. It looked like a grimace.

And if Max didn't like the paint on Diablo, Mrs. Reg was going to *hate* it.

Lisa was so despondent about the week's events that she barely noticed when Carole appeared at the door to Diablo's stable and perched a bottle of apple juice where Lisa could reach it.

"That stuff's really coming out, isn't it?" Carole asked, looking at the paint.

Lisa stopped her brushing and combing for a moment and looked at Diablo. The bay still looked more red and white than he ought to, but there was a fair amount of paint and paint-covered hair in the curry comb. Perhaps one day, in the not-too-distant future, the horse would once again be pure bay.

Lisa shrugged in answer to Carole's question. The fact that some of the paint was coming out didn't feel like much consolation.

"Look, as long as Stevie's taking care of Starlight for me, I'm going to run an errand for us," Carole said. "Dad told me he wouldn't get to the store to buy the food for our vegetable lasagna tonight, so I brought the recipe with me. I'll go over to the shopping center and get the stuff."

Lisa had completely forgotten about their dinner. She'd been so focused on Mrs. Reg's return and what *wasn't* going to get done by then that she hadn't remembered that there would be life after that. In fact she couldn't believe Carole could think about anything but the missing pin.

"You're really going shopping?" Lisa asked.

"I know it seems odd," Carole said. "I was thinking the same thing you're thinking now, but the fact is, worrying doesn't change anything. It won't help us to find the pin." It seemed like a wise philosophy. It didn't change any facts, but it did change the way Lisa felt about the facts.

"All right," she said. "You do the shopping, and when Stevie and I are done, we'll try to find the pin one more time. By then all the kids will be gone. We'll go back to the locker area. I know we combed every inch of it, but it's still the most logical place."

"Good idea," Carole said. "I'll cross my fingers for you."

Lisa returned her attention to Diablo's coat. Carole was right. The paint really *was* coming out.

HALF AN HOUR later Stevie and Lisa were once again on their hands and knees in the locker area. Stevie had found two flashlights, so the girls were peering under everything they could, sweeping every inch of the floor with beams of light, hoping to spot the glint of gold, the sparkle of a diamond.

"Very interesting," Veronica diAngelo said.

Lisa jerked upward, knocking her head on the bench she'd been looking under. Stevie just grunted and kept on looking.

"It's just two blind mice now, and they aren't sweeping, cleaning, painting, or trying to do everything else under the sun to butter up the stable manager and her son, are they?"

There was a cruel edge to her voice, and Lisa didn't like it at all. It was sharper and more painful than the dull ache in her head where she'd bonked herself against the bench. She just stared at Veronica and waited for her to go on.

"So I've been asking myself, what is all this about? And now, with the two of you on your hands and knees at my feet, I think I know."

She couldn't possibly know, Lisa told herself.

"It's the pin," Veronica said. "When you called me at home, I began to think about it. I knew I'd seen it before and it wasn't Stevie's. It took me a while to remember, but a pretty piece of jewelry like that will stick in a girl's mind, even when she's been told that it's a fake. The only other time I saw that pin, Mrs. Reg was wearing it. It's not a fake. It's real gold, with a real diamond. And you lost it, didn't you?"

Lisa's jaw dropped. That was enough of an answer for Veronica. "Just as I thought," she said.

"You're the one who threw it at the cat!" Lisa blurted out.

"Me?" Veronica asked. "No way, dear. I never even had the thing in my hand. You just showed it to me, don't you remember?"

No, that wasn't the way Lisa remembered it. Not at all. But it didn't matter. Even the fact that Veronica probably *did* throw it at the cat didn't change the fact that Mrs. Reg had permitted Lisa to show the pin to her friends, and Lisa was responsible for whatever happened to it. Arguing with Veronica wasn't going to change that situation.

"Why don't you just go home and gloat?" Stevie asked.

"Oh, I wouldn't think of it," Veronica said. "Why would I want to go home and gloat when I can stay here and do the same thing? This way I get to watch the demise of Max's precious three favorite riders—the girls who have been trying to make themselves look so good all week just to make up for the fact that they've done something unforgivable. No, Stevie, I wouldn't leave here right now for the world! In fact, I think I'll just sit here on the bench for a while and watch the two of you sweat. I don't get many opportunities to do that. I'm not going to miss this one."

With that, Veronica settled herself on the bench and watched.

There was very little to watch, though, because even the most careful search of every square inch of the locker area revealed only a few dust bunnies. No horses, no gold, no diamonds.

13

CAROLE PUT THE two bags of groceries on the bookshelf next to Mrs. Reg's desk. She hadn't even greeted Lisa and Stevie, who were sitting in Mrs. Reg's office, because the two of them looked so glum that there didn't seem to be anything worth saying.

Instead she was greeted with a recapitulation of Stevie and Lisa's talk with Veronica. That made Carole feel just as cheerful as her friends. It even made her lose her appetite for vegetable lasagna.

"I think I know what I'm going to say to Mrs. Reg," Lisa said.

"You've thought up a way to explain the mess we've made?" Stevie asked.

"Well, I haven't figured out everything I'm going to say, but it's going to begin with the words 'I'm sorry.'"

"That sort of covers it, doesn't it?" Carole remarked. "Beginning, middle, and end."

"Very sorry," Stevie concurred.

A car pulled into the driveway at Pine Hollow. The girls couldn't even bring themselves to look. They knew what it was and who it was. Max had picked his mother up at the airport. That was Max and Mrs. Reg. Now it was official that they couldn't hide the fact that the pin was missing and they'd made nothing but dreadful mistakes ever since Mrs. Reg left, all in the name of trying to make up for the unforgivable.

"Oh, no," Lisa said. "I think I've forgotten my speech."

"It starts with 'I'm sorry,'" Stevie reminded her. "And if you forget, we'll say it for you."

They were quiet then, quiet enough to hear Mrs. Reg's exclamation from out front.

"Why, this is *beautiful!*"

"What's that, Mother?" Max asked.

"The front of the stable! You painted it!"

"I did?"

"Well, somebody did," Mrs. Reg said. "Who else would do it?"

"Oh, that's right. Stevie, Lisa, and Carole decided

to paint it. I don't know why—and they also took a turn at painting Diablo while they were at it!" He laughed.

Glumly Lisa thought it would probably be the last time he would laugh for a long time.

"Well, where are these girls who think they can replace me?" Mrs. Reg asked.

"I think they're waiting in your office," Max said.

The Saddle Club stood up to welcome Mrs. Reg respectfully. She almost ran into her office and gathered the girls in her arms for a big welcoming hug. It was not exactly what any one of them was expecting. They hugged her back.

"The front of the stable looks just great! When Morris sees how much better it looks, he's going to love doing the painting for our living room! Don't you think so, Max?"

Max looked a little confused and then seemed to remember something. "Definitely," he agreed.

"Whatever made you decide to take on that job?" Mrs. Reg asked.

"It was on your list," Stevie said. "It said to paint the front of the stable."

"No, it didn't," Mrs. Reg said. "Or maybe it did, but that wasn't what I meant."

"Did we mess up again?" Lisa asked.

"Again?" Mrs. Reg answered. "This wasn't a mess-up. This was a case of mind reading. See, my old friend Morris Halpern is coming tonight, and he's staying with us for the weekend. He is an artist, and he offered to do a painting of the stable for our home. I was planning to ask him to spruce the place up a little bit in his painting, but now I don't have to. He can make the painting look just like the place. Thanks!" Then she turned to her son. "Max, didn't you even look at that list?" she asked. "Did you just let these girls do absolutely *everything?*"

Max shrugged sheepishly. "They seemed to be doing a pretty good job of it," he said. "Actually, I came in here last night and took a look at the chart Carole made for assigning horses, and I was very impressed with it. You have to get her to show you how she did it. I think you'll want to use that chart, too. Can you show her, Carole?"

"Well, sure," Carole said. "But—"

"No buts," Mrs. Reg said. "Because if you've gotten as good at assigning horses as Max said, you may just end up with that job permanently."

"Oh, no thank you," Carole said quickly, her mind suddenly filled with images of frantic riders all demanding gentle but spirited horses at the same time.

"I'm sure Mrs. Reg does a much better job of it than I ever could."

Max smiled knowingly at her. Everyone appreciated that that was a tricky job. "Well, that may be true, Mother, but the fact is that these girls have been working some magic around here in your absence."

The Saddle Cub was more than a little surprised to hear Max say that. He'd been so busy since his mother departed that they had barely seen him, and they didn't think he'd noticed anything—except the paint on Diablo. He hadn't even noticed that the front of the stable had been painted!

There was a knock at Mrs. Reg's door then. Everybody turned to see that it was Veronica diAngelo.

"Can I speak to you and Mrs. Reg for a minute? In private?" she asked. Stevie, Lisa, and Carole knew what was coming. It was inevitable, and they didn't like it at all.

"Not right now," Max said, granting the girls an unexpected reprieve. "My mother just got back. Can it wait until morning?"

"It's important."

"A little later then," Max said. Then he turned to his mother. "And you should have heard what some of the other riders said about these three."

The Saddle Club was not eager to hear this. Carole thought of the basketball players and the ponies, then she thought of Mr. Jarvis and the painted horse. Lisa thought only of Mr. French, the non-French non-ambassador.

"My phone's been ringing off the hook," Max said.

Stevie wasn't surprised. Of course there had been complaints.

"We've got a whole basketball team that wants to learn to ride. Apparently their coach told them that horseback riding would help their balance. So four of them came and tried it. They loved it. I don't know what these three girls did, but the players just couldn't stop talking about how wonderful all the riders were at the place and how much they loved the horses that had been assigned to them."

Mrs. Reg beamed. Lisa was sure it was the last smile she'd see on her face for a long time once Veronica got a word in edgewise. "It's awfully nice to know that when I'm gone, my shoes can be filled by young riders Max and I have trained so well."

"I guess we did," Max said. "But I can't claim any credit for the French lesson that one of these young riders delivered. A new rider here said he never had more fun or learned more on a trail ride than he did with Lisa. He said something about having a friend who wants to learn Arabic and wondered if we had any Arabian horses. I don't know what he was talking about, but he signed up for six months' worth of trail riding. For that, I'll learn Urdu! I don't know what you did, Lisa, but thank you."

"It's a long story," Lisa said, stunned. "But you're welcome."

"Max—I need to talk to you *now*."

"Not now, Veronica." Max turned back to his mother. "Then there's the case of Mr. Jarvis. That man is quite strange, you know."

"Oh, right," Mrs. Reg said, remembering. "I never knew what to make of his passion for pintos. It's always been tricky having Patch available for him. When is he coming back? I have to make a note so Patch will be free."

"He'll be back, all right, but he doesn't have to ride Patch. Our friend Carole managed to convince him to try a bay. He says he enjoyed the experience so much, he wants to try to ride every horse in the stable. Can you imagine? Another magic trick from our young riders."

"I'm just thrilled," Mrs. Reg said. "I had a wonderful visit with my friend, you know—and she's much better now. She just needed some cheering up. Anyway, when I didn't hear from Max, I knew everything was going smoothly. Good work."

"I'm not done, Mother," Max said. "I also had a call today from the man at Connor's. You know how difficult he can be. Well, it turns out that Stevie here somehow managed to do him a gigantic favor, and he says he's going to give us a ten percent discount on our next order."

"Great! We'd better make it a big one, then, right?"

"Good idea," Stevie said, keeping a straight face. "And trust me, they're prepared for it to be big—very big."

"Good, but what were you doing ordering grain? I thought we—"

"Max, *now*."

"Just a minute, Veronica. Can't you see my mother hasn't even taken her coat off?"

She hadn't. In fact, Max and Mrs. Reg had been so busy going over all the wonderful things The Saddle Club had been doing in their own unique way that Mrs. Reg hadn't even sat down. Max put down his mother's suitcase and reached to help her off with her raincoat. And when her raincoat came off, the girls couldn't believe their eyes.

For there, fastened securely to Mrs. Reg's blue

blouse, was a solid gold pin of a horse with a diamond for an eye.

There was stunned silence. Even Veronica couldn't think of anything to say.

"Your pin—" Lisa uttered finally.

"I always wear it when I'm dressed up," Mrs. Reg said. "Though, of course, it doesn't belong in a stable. I mean, look what happened last time I had it here. You girls did a wonderful thing by calming Prancer. I had to rush after I picked up the pin where you left it for me in the locker area, so I never had a chance to tell you how proud I was of the job you were doing. But I'm sure Max remembered to tell you, didn't he?"

"Max?" Stevie said.

"You *did* remember, didn't you?" Mrs. Reg asked accusingly.

Max looked downright sheepish. That was enough of an answer.

"You mean he never told you that I got the pin?" Lisa shook her head.

"I certainly hope you weren't worried about it," Mrs. Reg said.

The girls looked at one another. Stevie shrugged for them all.

Mrs. Reg turned squarely to her son. "Max Regnery," she began. "Is it possible that you knew that these girls were worried sick about my pin and you didn't tell them, just because you knew they'd be trying to do everything in the world to find it and to try to make up for losing it?"

"Why, Mother!" he said. "How could you suggest such a thing?"

One of the things about having really close friends was that sometimes, without a word or look passing among them, they all had the same thought. At that instant three minds conceived of the idea that Mrs. Reg was going to have a few stories to tell her son about horses and riders who used to be at Pine Hollow. And there was a chance, just a chance, that one of them was going to be about a farrier in a three-legged race. . . .

The girls had to get out of Mrs. Reg's office before they started laughing uncontrollably.

"Veronica, what is it you wanted to say to us?" Max asked, now desperately trying to change the subject.

"Nothing," she said darkly, and then spun on her heels and marched out of the office.

The Saddle Club was close behind.

14

THREE VERY TIRED, but very relieved and very happy, girls piled into the back of Colonel Hanson's station wagon.

"Time for a Saddle Club meeting!" Stevie announced as soon as the door slammed.

"I can't believe it!" Lisa said. "We got away with *everything*!"

"We are something!" Carole agreed. "Never was there a threesome like us!"

"What is going on?" Colonel Hanson asked.

"Oh, Dad, you won't believe what just happened!"

"Probably not," he agreed, "but I've come to learn that when the three of you get together to try to solve a problem, it gets solved and stays solved, and even after it's long gone and done, people often can't figure out exactly what happened."

"That's a perfect description!" Stevie said.

The three of them started laughing all over again. It was a very different laughter from the sort of desperate giggles they'd all had the day before. Now they were laughing with relief and joy. Each felt the wonderful strength of their friendship that seemed to make The Saddle Club greater than the sum of its parts.

"This is all fine and good," Colonel Hanson said, interrupting their celebration. "But didn't I hear something about vegetable lasagna this morning at the breakfast table? I don't see any signs of grocery bags, and we don't want to go to the supermarket at this hour. What happened?"

"Oh, that's almost the best of all!" Carole said. "See, we were on our way out of Mrs. Reg's office when she spotted the grocery bags. I *did* do the shopping, Dad. Anyway, she said something like 'Max, you remembered!' It turns out that when she put 'Food for Friday' on her list, she didn't mean that we should order grain and hay, she meant that her friend, the one who is going to do the painting of Pine Hollow—and that's another story—is coming for dinner, and she wanted to be sure she had something to cook for him.

She was even thrilled that he'd included a recipe for vegetable lasagna. She's been meaning to try it for months!"

Even Colonel Hanson had to start laughing then. "There seems to be no end to the trouble you three can get into and out of at exactly the same time, and I have no end of admiration for this wacky skill you have. Still, I want to know, what are you girls going to make me for dinner?"

Carole patted her jeans pocket. She had the change from her grocery shopping, and she had the money Max had handed her to pay her back for the groceries. It was way too much money for the groceries, but it wasn't too much for what she had in mind.

"Simple, Dad. We're going to make reservations!"

Everybody agreed that it was a great idea. They had a victory to celebrate.

ABOUT THE AUTHOR

BONNIE BRYANT is the author of more than fifty books for young readers, including novelizations of movie hits such as *Teenage Mutant Ninja Turtles* and *Honey, I Blew Up the Kid*, written under her married name, B. B. Hiller.

Ms. Bryant began writing The Saddle Club in 1986. Although she had done some riding before that, she intensified her studies then and found herself learning right along with her characters Stevie, Carole, and Lisa. She claims that they are all much better riders than she is.

Ms. Bryant was born and raised in New York City. She lives in Greenwich Village with her two sons.